Shop Till You Drop

"Nancy!" Bess cried as I reached her. Stretching her hand to me, she added, "Hey, could you give me a lift?"

"Why not?" I joked as I pulled her up. Once I'd made sure Bess was okay, my gaze flew to Swoon 2's window—smashed to smithereens. And still the women surged ahead, making for the narrow bottleneck of the door, as if clothes mattered more than whether someone might be hurt. "Can you believe it, Bess? They broke the window! I hope everyone's okay."

"This situation is lethal," Bess said in a shaky voice. "Let's get out of here if we can."

But Bess and I weren't going anywhere. The pressing mob made sure of that.

NANCY DREW
girl detective™

Available from Aladdin Paperbacks

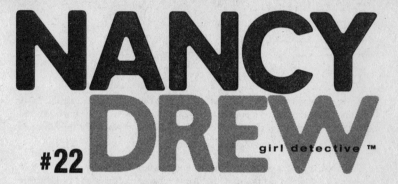

NANCY DREW

girl detective ™

#22

Dressed to Steal

CAROLYN KEENE

Aladdin Paperbacks
New York   London   Toronto   Sydney

This book is a work of fiction. Any references to historical events, real people, or real locales are used fictitiously. Other names, characters, places, and incidents are the product of the author's imagination, and any resemblance to actual events or locales or persons, living or dead, is entirely coincidental.

❧ ALADDIN PAPERBACKS
An imprint of Simon & Schuster Children's Publishing Division
1230 Avenue of the Americas, New York, NY 10020
Copyright © 2007 by Simon & Schuster, Inc.
All rights reserved, including the right of
reproduction in whole or in part in any form.
NANCY DREW is a registered trademark of Simon & Schuster, Inc.
ALADDIN PAPERBACKS, NANCY DREW: GIRL DETECTIVE, and
colophon are trademarks of Simon & Schuster, Inc.
Manufactured in the United States of America
First Aladdin Paperbacks edition February 2007
10 9 8 7 6 5 4 3 2 1
Library of Congress Control Number 2006932238
ISBN-13: 978-1-4169-3385-4
ISBN-10: 1-4169-3385-9

Contents

Dressed to Steal

A Lonely Road

I need a new dress," George said in a resigned tone. My friend George Fayne and I were on our way home from this fancy reception at the Maloney Community Center honoring Dad's twenty-year career as an attorney in River Heights. "No, make that several new dresses," George went on as I navigated a curve on a dark deserted stretch of road where deer have been known to pounce on cars. "I mean, I felt really out of it tonight in the clothing department. Gray—what was I thinking?" She stared down at her silky silvery sun dress with an expression of disgust. "This dress is so over."

"It's a great dress, George. What's not to like about it?" I asked, wondering what alien had kidnapped my friend and sent this girl in her place. George usually didn't give a second thought to her clothing.

"Everything. All the people at your dad's party looked as if they were practicing for the Oscars, and what was I wearing? Gray."

"*Silver*."

"That's a nice way of saying gray," George said. "Sorry if I'm sounding grumpy. It's just that tonight was such a special event, and I wanted to look my best."

"You looked awesome, George. And what does it matter, anyway? You were there to honor Dad, and he really appreciated that. He doesn't pay attention to what people are wearing—just what they're saying." I sneaked a glance at George. Usually, she never cares about superficial stuff like what people are wearing, either. Like Dad, she cares about people themselves— and maybe their ability to run the hundred-yard dash. George is totally into sports. I'm not kidding when I say she's a star athlete dreaming of an Olympic future.

"But do guys even notice clothes?" George mused. "Women sort of dress up for the benefit of each other, don't you think? Like tonight, Bess wore a cool purple strapless gown with pink flowers at the waist. And Deirdre was wearing that weird gold fluted gown that looked like a toga. But do you think Ned will remember what you wore, Nancy? I mean, he noticed you looked great, of course—but not the details, right?"

I had to agree with George. Ned Nickerson, my boyfriend, cares tons about me, and he's always had a weakness for my blue eyes. But tonight, had he noticed that I wore my blue and white sundress—the same one I've thrown on a zillion times when the two of us have gone out? Doubt it.

"Actually, George, I could use a new dress, too." I caught her raised eyebrow before I looked back at the road, checking the dark borders for roaming deer. Leafy green branches swayed in the breeze.

My mind drifted back to our talk. "Hey, how come we've spent more time in the past ten minutes on clothes than we have in the whole past year?"

George shrugged. "I don't know why. You're the detective!"

True enough. I spend a lot of my waking moments nosing around in places I shouldn't and solving mysteries that stump the police. No wonder I have no time for clothes. So why were George and I even having this conversation? I said, "Maybe we're obsessing on this subject because we wore old dresses to this glitzy party honoring Dad, with all his friends and clients, and we feel bad about that."

"And now we want to change our lives!" George quipped.

"Or at least our wardrobes. Maybe we should get advice from Bess—she definitely knows her stuff.

Like when she dragged us into Alicia Adams's store in Chicago last winter on our way to the museum. Remember how Bess bought tons of stuff while you and I bought nothing, and we barely made it to the museum before it closed? But she gave us lots of good advice."

George chuckled. "That we didn't use. Hey, didn't she buy the dress she wore tonight at that store?"

I cast my mind back to that freezing cold day in the Windy City—the warm cosy store, the friendly owner, and Bess all excited about her new clothes. A vague image of purple silk flashed across my brain. "I think you're right, George. That was the same dress. Good memory."

I always marvel at how different George and Bess are from each other, even though they're cousins and close friends themselves. Blond Bess is a clothes horse, while dark-haired George would rather be riding a real horse than shopping. Bess is short while George is taller than I am, and I'm five foot seven. But Bess and George do have a few things in common. Take machines. Bess is an ace car mechanic, while George is a computer whiz. They're equally loyal, smart, and brave. And last but not least, they both make crack assistant detectives.

Anyway, George and I should have known better than to allow Bess to sidetrack us from our mission of seeing a show at The Art Institute of Chicago. But I was glad we'd let Bess have her way. Otherwise, we wouldn't have met Alicia, the hot new fashion designer who grew up in our very own hometown, River Heights. Seeing Alicia's excitement about her new store, Swoon, and its success was inspiring.

"It's amazing how famous Alicia has become," George commented. "She has her designs all over the place—Paris, New York, Chicago, you name it."

"Charlie Adams is so proud of her," I said. "Whenever I take my car into his garage for a tune-up, he can't stop talking about his big sister. I know all about her. She left River Heights when she was eighteen—our age—to make it as a model in Paris. That was ten years ago."

"I can see why she'd make a good model," George said. "She's really gorgeous."

"But apparently she wasn't that happy with her job. The constant focus on looks got old quickly, so she came to Chicago, to the Fashion Conservatory. It's a really prestigious school if you want to design clothes. Anyway, that's what Charlie told me."

George shot me a sly look. "Nancy, have you ever wondered how many younger brothers talk that much about their older sisters? I'm sure my little brother doesn't go on about me like that. Sometimes I think Charlie has a crush on you. That's why he always bails you out when you run out of gas."

I tend to run out of gas when my mind is on a mystery. When I get going on a case, I'm like a dog with a bone. I can't put it down until I've solved the mystery, even if that means forgetting everything else in my life, including my gas tank.

But I couldn't use the mystery excuse tonight. As I glanced at the gas gauge, my heart sank. The needle was at the bottom of the red danger zone.

The wind whipped up, tossing tree boughs in the woods on either side of us. The enormous trees were like soldiers at arms, blocking the sky, which was dark and moonless anyway. George grinned at me, cheerful and oblivious, probably thinking of Charlie Adams. I bit my lip. Why get her started when there was every chance we'd make it to Vernon Avenue, near George's house, where there was an all-night gas station on the corner?

My mind clicked back to Alicia Adams, safely off the no gas topic. I said, "Charlie told me that after Alicia graduated from the Fashion Conservatory of Chicago, she went back to Europe to make it as a fashion designer. She lived there awhile, struggling to get recognized, and then, finally, success hit. By the time she moved to New York a few years later, her label was all over the stores and everyone loved her stuff."

"Awesome. So what happened in Europe that made Alicia's designs so popular suddenly?"

"Well, she had a good publicist," I explained, "and probably some decent luck. But mainly, her designs are incredibly original—don't you think? At a time when everyone was wearing black, Alicia's clothes were colorful and eye-catching. Charlie said the fashion writers used the word 'bold' to describe her."

"'Bold'—I like it," George declared. "So when did she move to Chicago?"

"Last year. She was excited about finding an affordable space to start her own store. Swoon features nothing but Alicia's own label. You saw her stuff, thanks to Bess. It's really trendy and cool. And Bess told me the other day that she's opening a branch, Swoon 2, in River Heights. It probably won't be open for another few weeks."

George grinned. "Bess can't stop talking about it. I tease her about the fact that she shares something with each Adams sibling: clothes and mechanics. Although Charlie and Alicia don't seem to share much in common with each other."

"Just that they're both friendly—and hard workers," I said. We drove in silence for a moment. Once more my eyes drifted to the zero balance in our gas tank.

Refocus!

"Hey, George, what do you say we revisit Swoon? This time, we won't let the museum distract us. If there's one thing this conversation has told me, it's that we both need new clothes. Why not give our business to a River Heights person? Or we could wait till Swoon 2 opens."

I sensed George's hesitation. Shopping just wasn't her bag.

"Come on, Fayne," I went on. "Let's bite the bullet and do a little shopping. It won't kill you. You started this subject, anyway. Remember your old gray dress?"

"Silver! Look, Nancy, I promise I'll shop with you someday. It's just that I'm busy for the next week with a lacrosse tournament."

A loud coughing noise drowned out George's lame excuse. *Uh oh.* I pressed my foot to the gas pedal, hoping I was hearing things, but the only response I got was another cough.

I felt the heat of George's gaze and turned toward it. Her brown eyes narrowed as we made eye contact. Funny—she didn't look the least bit surprised.

"I'm really sorry, George," I said as my trusty hybrid sputtered onto the road's shoulder and gave one final sad cough before stopping beside a cluster of dark evergreens.

"Out of gas again!" George exclaimed.

"Yes, but the good news is I managed to steer the car safely off the road."

"And the bad news is the road," George said. "It's dark and lonely. Where are we, anyway?"

"Not too far from civilization," I said brightly, although come to think of it, I hadn't seen a car pass us for the past ten minutes. "We couldn't be more than a mile from the residential part of River Street. A quick right onto Vernon Avenue will bring us to that all-night gas station a few blocks from your house."

"I don't recognize this spot at all," George said doubtfully. "If we were that close to my house, I'd know it." She sighed. "Now what, Nan?"

"We walk. It shouldn't be too far." I spoke boldly, and for good reason. After all, we weren't lost in the wilderness. We were on a road leading to the main drag of River Heights. George and I, on the track of various mysteries, had experienced much worse.

But as we stood outside the car, contemplating the dark, lonely trudge ahead, the wind whistled through the trees, blowing gusts of damp air in our faces. Clouds darker than the night itself scudded across the moonless sky. Obviously, a storm was about to hit us hard.

George grabbed my arm as a roaring sound burst through the silence. "What's that noise?"

9

"Get back!" I shouted. We jumped behind my car as a pickup truck zoomed by us, its cargo rattling, only to be swallowed again by the night.

The engine slowed, then stopped somewhere not far ahead of us. I stiffened, hoping the driver was a good Samaritan. Because if he or she wasn't, we might be needing one. I mean, it was really dark and lonely out here.

Lightning sliced the sky, spotlighting a man's dark silhouette walking toward us. I couldn't see much in the darkness, except George's worried glance.

2

Fun News

N ancy!" The voice was familiar. And when its owner materialized out of the darkness, George and I traded knowing grins. Charlie Adams, what a coincidence! I should have recognized his pickup truck's signature rattle.

"We must be psychic, Nancy," George muttered. "We talk about a person, and the next time we need him, he appears."

"Car trouble?" Charlie asked when he reached us. I opened my mouth to explain our predicament when he added, "You don't even have to tell me, Nancy. You're out of gas."

I shot him a grin. "No big deal, Charlie. I'm used to it by now."

"Me too."

If it hadn't been so dark, I could have sworn that a faint blush appeared under the stubble on his cheeks.

"So, Charlie, do you have any gas stashed in your truck?" George asked, cutting to the point.

Charlie chuckled. "I'll end the suspense right now, ladies." Turning, he strode back to his truck, then returned within seconds holding a gas can. As he filled up my tank, the conversation turned to Alicia. "Bess wore a dress tonight that your sister designed," I told him. "It turned heads at the party."

"Yeah, Alicia knows her stuff," Charlie replied proudly. Finishing with the gas, he added, "Hey, have you girls heard the news?"

"News?" I asked, perking up.

"Alicia's new store, Swoon 2, is opening on Friday. The painters finished earlier than expected. She's promising a huge one-day discount to celebrate."

"Charlie, that is so cool," I said. "I can't wait. Make that we can't wait." I nudged George. "See, George? You can get a beautiful dress on sale. Now you have no excuse for partying in an old one."

"Yes I do—my lacrosse game," she countered, and grinned. "You and Bess will just have to go to Alicia's sale without me."

I met Bess at the Moonbeam Diner the next day for lunch. "Hey," I said, sitting down opposite her at a booth. "I've got news." I told her about Swoon 2.

Bess gaped at me. "A sale, Nancy? That rocks. Alicia's stuff is normally so expensive. I used up all my hard-earned babysitting money on that dress I wore last night!"

"Worth every penny," I said. "You looked great, Bess. You definitely outshone Deirdre, that's for sure." Deirdre Shannon is a former classmate of ours. Though Deirdre has good qualities—intelligence and ambition—she also has a full blown case of egomania. She's never liked me or my friends, and Bess claims that's because she's jealous of my detective skills. Who knows? Even I can't figure out that mystery.

Bess's blue eyes lit up at my compliment before a doubtful expression crossed her face. "You'll come with me to the sale, right Nancy? George, too?"

"No George, unless we kidnap her from her lacrosse game."

"Forget George," Bess said, dismissing her cousin with a wave of her hand.

At six that evening, I kept an ear out for the doorbell. I'd invited Ned over for dinner. He never turns down a chance to eat Hannah's amazing roast chicken, his favorite dish. Hannah Gruen, our housekeeper, has lived with Dad and me since my mother died—when I was a mere three years old. *Housekeeper* is really the wrong word to describe Hannah. She's more like a member of our family.

Fifteen minutes later, over roast chicken, Ned said, "Nancy, I've got some news for you. Well, maybe you've already heard it."

"You mean about Alicia's sale?" I asked.

His face fell. "I was hoping to surprise you. But I should have known you'd heard since the whole town can't stop talking about it. The news has taken River Heights by storm."

"I actually surprised Bess with the news earlier," I said, helping myself to a platter of garlic beans, another of Hannah's specialties.

"The publicity snowballed this afternoon," Ned told me. "Oh, and guess what? Deirdre is going to be covering the opening for *Threads*. Of course, Natalie Stephanoff, our lead reporter, will be supervising her, but still. Deirdre did everything she could short of blackmail to make sure she got that assignment."

Ned and Deirdre were both interning at *Threads*, a fashion magazine in River Heights, Ned in the photography department for college credit, and Deirdre because her cousin, the managing editor, got her the job and Deirdre has always wanted to see her name in print. "So will you get to cover it too, Ned?" I asked.

Ned pushed his brown hair from his forehead and

smiled. "I'm the photographer's assistant. It's my first important assignment. Hope it goes okay."

I smiled. "I'm sure it will."

The next day, Thursday, George, Bess, and I grabbed some pizza before the movies. While waiting to be served, I said, "I'm actually getting worried that the sale might be a mob scene. Everyone is talking about it. I told Ned not to worry—that his photos of Alicia's opening would be awesome. But I hope he'll be able to get some."

"Oh, it'll be a mob scene," George said after taking a sip of her soda. "Even if I didn't have my lacrosse game, I wouldn't go. How can you shop with the whole town inside the store?"

Bess threw up her hands. "You guys, what an attitude! Am I the only positive thinker at this table? The sale will go just fine. It's all day long, and people will come at different times. Anyway, the important thing is that we'll be able to get amazing clothes at fire-sale prices. Who cares if there's a crowd?"

George and I exchanged looks as Bess went on. "Anyway, I'd appreciate some advice on my selections from friends I trust," she added firmly.

A pang of guilt shot through me. After all, I'd told Bess I'd come with her, and despite my misgivings, I couldn't let her down. And truthfully, I didn't mind going. I was curious to see what the fuss was about. "Don't worry, Bess," I said. "I wouldn't let you down. What time does the store open?"

Promptly at eleven o'clock the next morning, Bess and I met outside Swoon 2 on River Street downtown—although *outside* is a polite way of saying at least a half a block from the store. George and I were dead right. It was a total mob scene.

"I can't believe this crowd," Bess said anxiously as a woman jostled her from behind. "I'm really sorry, Nancy. I never believed it would be anything like this."

"Don't worry about it, Bess. I was curious to see this event anyway. It's more than just a sale—it's a piece of River Heights history."

"I hope we both survive it without getting trampled," Bess added. "This crowd looks lethal."

I had to agree. The vast majority of the mob was women, with the exception of a few police officers making fruitless attempts at crowd control. Impatient yells filled the air, directing the store to open immediately since it was past eleven, the time advertised for the sale. There was no organized line that I could see, just a mass of women thronging the sidewalk and street, which had been closed to traffic by the police. Standing on tiptoe, I could barely make out the tiny storefront with its gold banner proclaiming SWOON 2 in cool black lowercase letters that resembled calligraphy.

"How will all these women fit into that tiny store?" I asked as an older woman dug her elbow into my side. "Ow! I don't know, Bess. I predict disaster. Why don't we cut and run? We can always come back later and still make the sale."

"Everything will be gone by then," Bess said gloomily. "Trust me—I know. These women are like locusts, stripping everything in their path. I think we should just take a step back and not panic. It won't be like some unruly rock concert. These women are more sophisticated than that."

"Sophisticated?" I squeaked, as a woman stepped on my toe. "Bess, you just said they were locusts. And I hope you weren't being literal when you said we should take a step back. There's no way to move in any direction."

"Which means we can't leave even if we wanted to," Bess said. "Nancy, I'm sorry—no way did you sign on for this. I owe you one."

I grinned at her. "Bess, you've helped me in so many dangerous situations when I've been on the track of a mystery. I'm the one who owes you."

"Well, you're paying now," Bess said grimly. "What was I thinking? This is *worse* than some crazy rock concert."

She was right. The crowd had suddenly taken on a life of its own. "Ouch!" yelled a woman on Bess's right.

"Don't push!" another one shouted in my ear. A sudden commotion in the direction of the store told me that the doors had finally opened. An electric charge seemed to zap the crowd, and it surged forward like some giant lumbering beast impossible to distract from its prey.

"Hey!" shouted a policeman who was manning the door. "That's enough shoppers inside at a time. Fire regulations." But his words were drowned out by the yelling crowd.

"The police are totally surprised by the size of this crowd," I shouted to Bess.

"The reporters, too," Bess replied. "See Ned?" She gestured in the direction of a white van; several reporters and photographers sat on its roof snapping pictures and scrawling notes, including Ned and Deirdre. Bess was right that the *Threads* gang looked surprised, but they also seemed eager, unlike the panicking police. The officer by the door had resorted to waving his arms at the shoppers like a broken windmill.

Meanwhile, the mob pressed forward. "You're hurting me!" a nearby woman shouted to someone next to her.

"Help!" someone else cried, her face filled with anguish.

"Nutcase!" a third person screamed. I shifted uneasily in my tight spot.

Suddenly the crowd went bonkers. Rude cries and screams of pain rang out everywhere as the crowd of women stampeded the tiny store.

"Nancy!" Bess screamed, reaching her hand out for mine. I stretched to catch it, but she was swept away by the mob.

"Nancy!" she screamed again.

"Bess, move to the edge of the crowd!" I yelled, but then she stumbled. My heart caught in my throat as she was sucked down like a person drowning. "Bess!"

The sound of shattering glass filled the noisy air.

3

Mobbed

Bess!" I called again, searching the stampeding crowd for a sight of her long blond hair.

Nothing.

I bit my lip, hoping she hadn't been crushed. And then I spotted her through a gap in the crowd, struggling to get up from her knees. I had to bridge the ten-foot gap between us, fast. "Coming through!" I yelled. The crowd didn't part easily, but thanks to my determination, I was able to push my way through to her. Under normal circumstances, I'd call myself rude, but these circumstances were *not* normal. I had to save Bess!

"Nancy!" she cried as I reached her. Stretching her hand to me, she added, "Hey, could you give me a lift?"

"Why not?" I joked as I pulled her up. Once I'd made sure Bess was okay, my gaze flew to Swoon 2's window—smashed to smithereens. And still the women surged ahead, making for the narrow bottleneck of the door, as if clothes mattered more than whether someone might be hurt. "Can you believe it, Bess? They broke the window! I hope everyone's okay."

"This situation is lethal," Bess said in a shaky voice. "Let's get out of here if we can."

But Bess and I weren't going anywhere. The pressing mob made sure of that. "Bess, look at the store," I said, pointing at a group of terrified shoppers trapped inside as the crowd prevented them from leaving through the door. Jagged pieces of glass poked up like shark's teeth where the picture window had been. The evil-looking glass might as well have been prison bars, keeping the inmates from fleeing.

Police sirens blared through what should have been a peaceful, sunny morning. Heads turned toward a squad car inching through the crowd. Slowly, glacially, the mob parted for the cops as they moved forward, admonishing people from a loudspeaker to get out of their way.

A gasp went up as an ambulance followed them. Several police officers charged through on foot, shouting through bullhorns for everyone to get back. Once the ambulance stopped, medics burst out with a stretcher, then elbowed their way into the store.

"Someone *was* hurt," Bess breathed. "I hope not seriously."

"It looks serious," I said as moments later the medics rushed back outside with a young woman on the stretcher. Her arm and shoulder were bound in bloody gauze, and her eyes were wide with shock as the medics slid her into the ambulance.

The crowd miraculously settled down at the sight of the injured woman. After a moment, a police officer stood on a bench and shouted through a bullhorn, "Swoon 2 is closed for the rest of the day. Depending on whether the window can be fixed, the store will reopen tomorrow at noon with timed tickets issued. Times will be assigned randomly to avoid a repeat of this situation. It will do you no good to hurry into a line to get an early ticket. The sale will last three days instead of one so there is no need to rush. I ask everyone's cooperation. We don't want another injury."

A collective sigh went up from the crowd. I couldn't tell whether people felt guilty at behaving so ridiculously, or whether they were disappointed that they might not get a bargain after all.

The crowd began to thin. "Check out Deirdre,"

Bess said, nodding in the direction of the white van. "She doesn't seem concerned that someone was hurt."

Bess was right. Perched on the roof of the white van, Deirdre was calmly jotting notes. Next to her, Ned and his boss clicked away with their cameras while a short woman with a halo of dark curls and a notepad fluttered among the crowd of women, chatting with people almost as if she were schmoozing at a party.

"Yes, but to be fair, Ned and his boss don't look that concerned, either," I said. "And neither does that dark-haired reporter."

"I guess that's just journalism," Bess said with a shrug. "It's their job to get the stories and pictures and hope the world cares. Besides, what could Ned do for the injured woman? Nothing. But maybe the pictures he snaps will raise awareness and get better crowd control for River Heights!"

"A worthwhile cause," I quipped. "By the way, Bess, do you know who that dark-haired woman is? The one who looks like she has an ego twice her size?"

"You mean Deirdre?" she answered mischievously. "No, I don't know who that short woman is, but since she's carrying a notepad, she's probably a reporter."

"I'll bet she's the lead reporter, Natalie something, Deirdre's boss. Ned mentioned her the other night."

"Nancy, look, there's Chief McGinnis," Bess said,

pointing to a tall police officer with bushy dark eyebrows and a large gut. As head of the River Heights Police Department, Chief McGinnis was sometimes my ally and sometimes my obstacle, depending on his mood and my powers of persuasion at the time. "He's going into the store. I hope Alicia's okay."

"I'm sure she could use some help," I said. "Why don't we see if we can get in."

"Sure," Bess said gamely. Weaving our way among the stragglers, we arrived at the door of Swoon 2, only to be met by a resolute looking Chief McGinnis, his arms crossed in front of him.

"Hey, no one goes inside," he barked.

"I'd love to search the store for evidence, in case a crime was committed," I said. "That would be a giant help to you guys, right Chief?"

"Nancy," he said wearily. "There's no crime here, other than sheer stupidity. The crowd thought they could fit inside this tiny store and figured that pushing someone through the window would get everyone in faster."

"But what if someone stole merchandise and Alicia doesn't realize it yet?" I countered. "I mean, who would notice a clever thief in such a zoo? Plus, we know Alicia. She's Charlie's sister, you know."

Chief McGinnis's dark eyebrows knitted together into one thick line as he scowled at me. I smiled back, and he sighed heavily, his shoulders relaxing. "Okay, fine. Go along inside. Maybe you can give poor Alicia some moral support. But be sure to report back."

Bess and I thanked him as we slipped past.

Once inside, we found two police officers sweeping shattered glass from the floor, and Alicia, by her cash register, struggling not to cry. Or not to cry again; her cheeks were already streaked with tears.

Even so, she was gorgeous. Slender and tall with a delicate china-doll face, Alicia had waist-length auburn hair splashing down her back, and her teardrop-shaped eyes were a cool, pale green color. They lit up the instant I called her name.

"Nancy, Bess!" she replied, crossing over to us. "Man, am I happy to see you. How did you get in?"

"I told Chief McGinnis I'd come to help," I said. "Alicia, I'm *so* sorry about your store."

"Thanks—so am I," she said, her shoulders sagging. I crossed my fingers she'd hold it together and not cry again—her emotions seemed almost as fragile as her appearance. "I'm horrified by what happened," she went on. "It was totally my fault. That woman was pushed into the window because I failed to supervise my publicity agent."

"Because what?" Bess said, gaping. "Alicia, this was *not* your fault."

"That's nice of you to say, Bess," Alicia replied

gravely, "but I'm afraid it was. See, I hadn't meant for my sale to get so much publicity. I knew the slightest advertising would cause a mob scene. Word-of-mouth would have been just fine, but somehow ads were placed in *Threads* and the *River Heights Bugle*, and the sale was mentioned on local radio thanks to some press releases they somehow received."

"Somehow?" I repeated, my mystery radar up. "You mean, your publicity agent didn't place those ads, or send out press releases?"

"She denies it," Alicia said, rolling her eyes. "But I don't believe her. Who else would have?"

Someone who wants to make trouble for Alicia? I kept my mouth shut, though. The last thing Alicia needed was more to worry about.

4

Creepy Crimes

I woke up Saturday morning with a bad feeling. There was something on my mind, which is why I woke so early—seven a.m. to be precise, a totally unnatural time of day for a teenager to be conscious. I didn't exactly have a headache. It was more as if some tiny annoying gnome was inside my head, tapping away with a blunt instrument, nagging me to remember something. And then suddenly yesterday's crazy events flooded back into my memory. No chance I could get back to sleep now.

After showering and dressing—blue jeans, a tank top, and sneakers, in case I had a full blown investigation on my hands—I sat down at the kitchen table, where Hannah was making blueberry pancakes, and filled her in on what had happened.

"Well, it doesn't sound like much of a mystery to me," Hannah said. I felt a pang of disappointment. I'd so welcome a new case, but maybe Hannah was right. Maybe I was getting my hopes up for nothing. After thanking Hannah for handing me a plate of pancakes, I countered, "But no one knows who leaked the sale to news outlets all over town. Alicia's publicist says she didn't, so I'm thinking someone might have it out for Alicia."

Hannah stopped, and looked at me. "Nancy, have you ever asked yourself whether you sometimes see mysteries where none exist? In this case, Alicia wasn't keeping the sale a real secret. She was depending on word-of-mouth for her customers; otherwise, she'd have no customers for her sale! Some customer could have innocently mentioned the sale to a friend who works for the *Bugle* or *Threads*. This is a pretty small town, after all. It wouldn't have to be someone who has it out for Alicia."

Spoken just like Hannah. She's one of the most sensible people I know. And she could be right. Still, my mystery radar detected something, and it was pretty accurate. Right now it was picking up tiny vibrations. And if my radar was wrong, this would be the first time.

"Hannah, I hope for Alicia's sake that you're right," I said as I put my plate in the dishwasher. "Still, I thought I'd head over to Swoon 2 before it opens and see if Alicia has anything more to report."

Hannah threw up her hands. "I just don't want you to be too disappointed if the mystery, well . . . isn't."

"Don't worry, Hannah," I said, giving her ample waist a generous hug. "If this isn't a mystery, I'll be sure to find another one sooner or later."

"That's what I was afraid you'd say," Hannah said affectionately. "Just be careful, Nancy, whatever the day holds for you."

After promising Hannah I would, I grabbed my backpack, jumped in my car, and headed downtown to Swoon 2. Dad and Hannah are always telling me to be careful. And I always am. But that doesn't mean I'm afraid of a challenge. In fact, just the opposite. I do whatever it takes to solve a mystery, and I deal with whatever danger that mystery throws my way— carefully.

Once I got to Swoon 2, I wasn't surprised to see Alicia already there, cleaning up the store. The window had been completely fixed, gleaming in the sun. "Nancy!" Alicia exclaimed, forcing a smile as I entered. Uh oh. Had something else gone wrong? Picking up a dress from the floor, her hands shook, and her long red hair had been swept up in a messy knot as if she hadn't had time to brush it. "What brings you here so early? It's only nine o'clock."

"I thought I'd see whether you needed any help." My stomach knotted as I added, "How is the woman who was hurt yesterday? Have you heard?"

"You mean Barbara Tsao? I called the hospital earlier and learned she's fine, due to be released later today. Thank goodness! That's a load off my mind."

"So what is on your mind, Alicia?" I asked gently. "I don't mean to pry, but you still seem upset."

Alicia's gaze slid from mine. "Is my mood so obvious, Nancy? I'm trying my best to put a good face on things, but yesterday just threw me for a loop. And then today, well . . . it's even worse."

"What happened, Alicia?" I asked, crossing over to her.

She held up a dress that had been draped over the glass counter by the cash register. My breath caught in my throat at the sight. The dress had once been gorgeous—peach silk with orange, pink, and yellow sequined ribbons flowing from the skirt. The exquisite sequined bodice had been ripped to shreds with scissors, and the skirt had been splashed with bleach. "My most expensive creation," Alicia said, crumpling it back on the counter. "Ruined. And that's not all," she added, gesturing toward a back wall. "Feast your eyes, Nancy."

I blinked in astonishment at the rude scrawls— black magic marker on an eggshell white wall—

behind a row of jackets. ANIMAL KILLER said one. DON'T THANK ME FOR MY HIDE said another. The last was the most ominous: I'LL SKIN YOU JUST LIKE YOU SKINNED ME.

My gaze flew to the jackets. They were fitted, stylish, and sporty, with fur-trimmed hoods. They'd keep a city dweller plenty warm, but they hadn't been designed for serious outdoor winter sports. The vandal probably thought the fur was more like an ornament than a necessity. "What kind of fur is that?" I asked.

"Coyote," Alicia replied. "But the coyotes aren't killed. I would never agree to that. I get the fur from a local keeper who trims it harmlessly. Anyway, I don't know how this vandal got into the store. A metal security gate protects the window, so it shouldn't have mattered that it had been broken. I've been here since seven a.m. with the window guys, cleaning up. So it happened during the night."

"Is anything missing?" I asked.

"Nope," Alicia said. "That's the only *somewhat* good news, aside from Barbara being okay."

I glanced around the store. The vandalism was disturbing, but what really struck me was that the rest of the store was in pretty good shape considering what could have happened. The window guys had done a great job, and except for the ruined dress and the anticruelty slogans that had been sprinkled in a small area, the store looked awesome. The beige carpet was all soft and plush, sleek chairs upholstered in colorful satins brightened the place, and on the racks, clothes gleamed like brilliant jewels.

"There's more good news, Alicia," I said, smiling. "Swoon 2 looks fantastic. People are going to love shopping here—as soon as you paint over those scrawls."

"And as soon as we figure out who's responsible for the vandalism so we can make sure it doesn't happen again," Alicia said firmly. "Which brings me to my next question. Charlie, my brother, tells me you're a detective, Nancy. You wouldn't be interested in, uh, investigating this for me, would you?"

"I thought you'd never ask!" I said, thrilled that my mystery radar was on target yet again. I knew a case when I saw it.

Relief washed over Alicia's heart-shaped face, and her entire body relaxed as she gave me a hug. "Thank you, Nancy, that's great," she said simply.

"Have you called the police about the vandalism?" I asked her, cutting to the chase.

"Not yet. I didn't want anything to distract the window repairmen. But I'll call Chief McGinnis before I open the store at noon. That is, if you think I should."

"Absolutely," I replied. "Just let me check out the place for clues before the police come. Oh, and don't paint over the scrawls until the police see them for evidence. In the meantime, do you have a big picture or a wall hanging to put up there? Something tells me shoppers won't think those messages go with the decor."

Alicia brightened. "Yes, I have a giant framed photo of me in my modeling days. It's in the back. It might be perfect in a store that's all about original fashion design. As long as I won't seem like an egomaniac, hanging pictures of myself."

"No Alicia, it'll be cool," I said reassuringly. As she went to get the photo, the store's cordless phone rang on the glass counter, and I picked it up. "Swoon 2. Can I help you?"

A man's rude voice barked into my ear. "You'll pay my daughter's medical bills, or I'll sue you big time!" A click, and then all was silence.

5

Mean Messages

I almost dropped the phone. Obviously that was Barbara Tsao's father, and he wasn't in a forgiving mood. Could he have had something to do with the vandalism? Maybe he wanted revenge for her injuries? Unlikely, but possible. Time to check out the store for clues.

After telling Alicia about the phone call and helping her hang the photo, I got to work. Once again, I was struck by how normal the store looked if you didn't count the hideous scrawls and mauled dress. Could someone have vandalized the place to distract from another crime?

The store was laid out with racks of clothes set along the walls at eye level, except for a spot where two armchairs had been placed. Above the armchairs was the only blank wall in the store, now covered with the scrawls and the photo; luckily for the vandal, the fur-trimmed jackets were directly to the right, so he could easily make his—or her—point. A circular rack stood in the center of the room, but the store had plenty of space for a person to walk around and eyeball the merchandise. The basic vibe of the place was cool and uncluttered.

So it was easy for me to spot something out of place, like the small white rectangular thing under the rack nearest the window. Scooting down, I pushed aside a gauzy lime colored skirt and picked up a business card. The name "Michael Tsao, Esq." in solid black print popped out at me. Barbara's father? Thanks to my own dad's profession, I knew that "Esq." stood for "Esquire," and meant this man was a lawyer.

I whipped my cell phone out of my backpack and speed-dialed Dad's office, where he'd gone early this morning to take care of some extra paperwork. Because Dad is so conscientious, he makes it his business to know his competition—which means every other lawyer in town. "Hey, Dad," I said after he answered. "Do you know a guy named Michael Tsao?"

"I sure do, Nancy," Dad said. "He's not my favorite attorney in River Heights, I'll say that."

"Really? Tell me about him."

"He encourages people to sue each other, even when the situation may not be ethical, and he's also unpleasant. But he almost always wins his cases. The few times I've faced him in court, I've won most of the cases, but I had to fight very hard for my clients. He's a tough opponent, and he resents that I've been successful against him most of the time."

"Do you think he's capable of revenge?" I asked.

"Maybe. Why? What are you involved with, Nancy?" Dad added, his voice registering concern.

I briefly filled him in on the case, then asked, "How is Mr. Tsao unethical?"

"Well, he's been known to follow ambulances after car crashes. Once the injured person is at the hospital, he'll pester them to sue the driver of the other car even when it's unclear who was at fault. If the accident didn't involve another person, he'll urge the person to sue the car company, even if the accident was the driver's fault. Those are just a few examples."

"Nice guy!" I exclaimed.

Dad chuckled, then said, "He and I do have one thing in common. Michael is a widower with a daughter living at home. She's a student at River Heights Law School. Barbara is her name, I think."

"Barbara," I repeated. My mind clicked back to the way the store had looked yesterday when Bess and I stopped in to help Alicia. My mental snapshot of it told me that Mr. Tsao's business card had not been under the rack then. He must have dropped it after the store had been locked up. No other people besides Bess and me had been allowed inside once the police took charge. What had seemed so unlikely now seemed possible—that he had trashed Swoon 2 in revenge for his daughter's injuries. Or maybe he'd hired some gangster to do his dirty work, and the person had dropped the card.

"I think I'll investigate him," I said absently, forgetting Dad might have a problem with that. He wouldn't want me messing with someone so nasty.

But all Dad did was to sigh deeply. "Okay, Nancy, just be careful." He knows me well enough to realize I can't be stopped.

"By the way, Dad, would you mind giving me the Tsaos' address?"

"I'll give it to you, but you must promise not to do anything that could anger him. I've witnessed his temper in court, and I wouldn't want it directed at you."

"I promise, Dad, and thanks!" I said as I jotted the address in my notepad.

Next call: the hospital. I learned that discharge time for patients was eleven. I checked my watch—

ten thirty. If I hurried, I could get to the Tsaos' house while they were still away.

After telling Alicia my plans and urging her to call the police, I left the store. Even though I was in a rush, I made time to pick up Bess and George. I wanted their company—and maybe their help.

"What if Mr. Tsao is home?" Bess asked, once the three of us were together in my car and I'd updated them on the case. "He might not have gone to the hospital to pick up Barbara."

"True," George said. "What if he's one of those rich, absent dads who shower their kids with stuff but never make time for them? Who knows? He might have sent one of his lackeys to pick up Barbara."

"I've already thought of that," I said. "If Mr. Tsao is home, we'll pretend to be law school classmates of Barbara's, concerned about her accident. In fact, what do you guys say we stop at a florist for some props?"

At exactly eleven, we pulled into the Tsaos' driveway off Shady Road, where a Jaguar convertible lounged in the sun like the jungle cat it was named for. The Tsaos' huge, showy mansion was set on a hill overlooking the river; two marble lions with scary snarling faces welcomed us from either side of the front door.

"I just hope Alicia's insurance company won't be

the next to fork over cash for Mr. Tsao's ritzy life-style," I murmured to George and Bess as I rang the doorbell.

The door opened immediately, and I steeled myself to face Mr. Tsao. Instead, a small plump maid with wavy blond hair, a starched black and white uniform, and suspicious eyes let us in. "Yes?"

"Uh, is Barbara here?" I asked. "We're law school classmates of hers, and we heard she had an accident."

She took the flowers from me without cracking a smile. "She's on her way home. Would you like to wait for her in the parlor?" She gestured toward a sunken living room filled with an assortment of chairs and sofas.

"Sure," I said, "that'd be great." The chair I sat in had gold armrests shaped like sphinxes. Bess and George chose a lavishly upholstered love seat.

"Let me get you some iced tea while you wait," she offered.

"Thanks," I said, and she headed off toward a swinging door that I guessed was the kitchen's. "We've got about two minutes till she comes back," I said to Bess and George. "I'm going to search Mr. Tsao's room for clues."

"In two minutes, Nancy?" Bess said. "Please hurry!"

"Just cover for me here, okay guys? I'll be, uh, in the bathroom."

"Good excuse," George said. "Now, get going and maybe I won't have to lie to her. She's a bit scary."

Once upstairs, I identified Mr. Tsao's room by the plaid bedspread, the suits in the closet, and the giant photograph of a heavyset dark-haired man—who else could it be but him?—taking up space on his bureau. It dwarfed the smaller one of him and his wife on their wedding day shoved in beside it.

Scanning the room, I wasn't even sure what kind of clues I was looking for. A black marker in a jacket pocket for scrawling slogans on the wall? A note with someone's phone number on it—the thug he might have hired? Anything that seemed out of place, I figured.

A sparkle caught my eye on the rug near his bed. Glitter? Not exactly Mr. Tsao's style. Stooping, I picked up several tiny pink and orange sequins, exactly like the ones on Alicia's ruined dress, and carefully put them in my jeans pocket. As I did, I caught sight of myself in the full length mirror on the opposite wall. Did I even look old enough for law school? Hmm. Might be a hard story to pass off. I checked my watch, which read eleven forty. We really should be going.

Back in the parlor, George and Bess were sipping iced tea nervously. George said, "We followed your advice, Nancy, and told the maid you were in the bathroom. She didn't seem quite as strict as before. Anyway, I don't think she suspected anything."

"Speaking of which, I found stuff," I said. "But I don't want to press our luck. Maybe we should just leave the flowers and split. At this point, running into Mr. Tsao might be counterproductive. Dad knows him, so there's a slight chance Mr. Tsao might recognize me."

"In that case, our law school aliases might get a bit awkward," George said.

"Plus," Bess added, "even if he doesn't recognize you, Nancy, it might not be in your best interest for him to know what you look like. Just in case you need to use a different alias with him sometime."

"Good point, Bess," I said. "Why give him information when we don't have to? Anyway, all I wanted from this visit was to learn whether he's worth considering as a suspect. And he definitely is. I'll tell you guys more about what I found when we're in the car."

I stuck my head through the swinging door, which lead into an elaborate pantry where I spotted the maid. "I wanted to thank you for the iced tea,"

I told her. "Unfortunately, we've got to go—to our, uh, contracts class. We were hoping Barbara would be back by now, but please tell her we hope she feels better." With a cheery wave, I shut the door before she had time to ask my name.

Once in the car, I told Bess and George about the sequins. "It's too suspect to be just a weird coincidence. Why would sequins be on the floor of a man's bedroom the day after Alicia's dress—which was the same color as the sequins—was torn up? His card suggests that Mr. Tsao may have been at the store, and we know he threatened to sue Alicia."

"But what do animal rights have to do with him?" Bess wondered. "He doesn't seem the type to care about cute furry creatures. What does coyote fur have to do with Barbara?"

George said, "Maybe he wrote the messages on the spur of the moment when he noticed the coyote fur. As a distraction, or maybe out of anger."

"Who knows?" I said. "Anyway, I want to show Alicia the sequins. She'd be able to tell me whether they came off that dress."

My friends had errands to do, so I dropped them off at their houses. Ten minutes later, I slid my hybrid into a parking place on River Street, a block away from Swoon 2. It was twelve thirty—the store had been open for half an hour.

Inside, a group of angry and confused customers buzzed around Alicia. "What's the meaning of this?" an older woman asked her, thrusting a piece of paper inches from Alicia's startled face. "What do you mean I've got blood on my hands?"

6

Wily Coyotes

strode over to the counter. "Can I help?" I asked. The woman, thin and middle-aged with frosted hair and one too many face-lifts, turned on me. Her fierce scowl acted like a force field. I stepped back.

"I'm not sure, *can* you?" she snapped, apparently mistaking me for a salesgirl. She thrust the piece of paper into my hands as Alicia shot me a grateful smile. Alicia had a hunted animal look about her, and who could blame her? This group of shoppers looked pretty scary with their flashing credit cards and loud demands. "This jacket was very expensive, and what do I get for my money? An insult!" the woman added.

I unfolded the piece of paper. It said, "You've got blood on your hands. PFAF."

Another woman, tall and skinny with spiky black hair, handed me hers. "Look!" she cried.

The note said, "Did I give you permission to wear my fur? Sincerely yours, Mr. Coyote. PFAF."

A girl my age with a spoiled pout read me hers. "Rip off more fur and Mr. Coyote will bite you big time. PFAF."

I looked at all three women. "Where did you get these?"

The first woman explained, "They were in the pockets of the coyote-fur jackets. I bought mine before discovering that vile message, and I want my money back!"

"Me too!" the dark-haired one said, while the pouting girl whined, "I haven't bought my jacket yet, but I think I should be paid for it anyway. Or get a free one. For my trauma and such."

"What's PFAF?" I asked, cutting into the sob stories.

"I'll look it up," Alicia said, and began to click on her computer monitor behind the counter. "Hmm," she added after a moment, "it's a local animal rights organization that stands for People For Animal Friends, run by a woman named Bettina Quintana."

"That woman ought to be jailed," the frosted blond said bitterly.

Peering at the screen, Alicia went on, "But why

would PFAF be targeting me? My fur is cruelty free. I get it from a local keeper who trims fur from live coyotes. He doesn't kill them. I'm very conscientious about that. Nancy, do you have a gut feeling about why PFAF would come after me?"

"I can't imagine why they'd be targeting you, Alicia," I replied, puzzled, "unless they don't realize that the fur comes from live animals. Assuming that PFAF is even responsible for this."

For a moment, Alicia looked thoughtful as she took in my words. Then, squaring her shoulders, she faced the three women. I was glad to see she was showing them some spirit.

"I'd be happy to issue refunds for your jackets if you don't like them," she said crisply. "We normally give store credit, but since this is a special situation, I'll agree to credit your cards. As for you," she added, turning to the girl, "I'm sorry you felt traumatized, but since you never actually bought the jacket, you're owed neither money nor merchandise."

The girl left in a huff, slamming the door behind her, while the women waited silently for Alicia to process their credits. After they'd left, Alicia said, "Once I get rid of the nasty notes in the rest of the pockets, those jackets will sell like hotcakes. Those women will be sorry, and they'll demand that I make them more." She shrugged. "You can't win."

"I couldn't do what you do, Alicia," I said admiringly. "Catering to those kinds of demands."

"Well, I couldn't do what *you* do, Nancy! Speaking of which, I bet you didn't come back here to fend off three evil shoppers. Do you have news?"

I fished Mr. Tsao's sequins from my pocket and placed them on the glass counter. "Look at these."

Her gaze flew to mine. "They're sequins from my dress! Where'd you find them?"

"On Michael Tsao's bedroom rug. You know, he's Barbara's dad?"

"How could I forget him? The man who wants to sue me for every penny I'm worth."

"The same. But I wonder how the sequins got on his rug. Could he have stepped on the dress while he was ripping it, and they scraped off on his carpet? Or maybe they got caught in the cuffs of his pants and fell out when he got undressed?"

"That's a great find, Nancy. Congratulations! If you ask me, it makes Mr. Tsao seem pretty suspicious. Oh, and I meant to tell you," Alicia said. "Something did go missing from the store after all."

I perked up. "What?"

"A pair of aquamarine stud earrings shaped like butterflies. I'd placed them close to the front of the glass jewelry display—an easy grab. The vandal must have found the key to the display in the drawer next to the register—a silly place for me to keep it. Now I know."

Earrings, huh? I turned my attention from Mr. Tsao back to Bettina Quintana, the leader of PFAF. Granted, Mr. Tsao struck me as very suspicious, but so did PFAF, which, apparently, hadn't done its research. Plus, if the vandal was Mr. Tsao, I wasn't sure how to explain the animal rights angle. Was he a crusader for animal rights as well as for accident victims? Somehow, I doubted it. Anyway, I don't like focusing on one suspect without considering other possibilities. Big mistake.

So, back to Bettina. Could she have stolen the earrings to sell them to raise money for PFAF? I asked Alicia, "Does PFAF give their address on the website?"

"Let me check," she replied, and a moment later she was jotting it down for me. After thanking her, I hurried to my car while speed-dialing Ned on my cell to bring him up to date on the case. Since it was Saturday, he didn't have work. What better companion to help me investigate PFAF headquarters? Besides being a supportive boyfriend, his gruffer voice might come in handy against any ferocious stray critters lurking about the place that PFAF might have rescued.

We hung up and I drove to Ned's house, where he persuaded me to get a bite of lunch before we set out on our mission. After sharing a BLT on a sesame roll, we were on our way, with me at the wheel of my hybrid, and Ned navigating.

PFAF headquarters was located on the second floor of an old loft building in a grimy manufacturing section on the edge of downtown. The weed-choked sidewalks were deserted, and there was no response when I rang the outside buzzer labeled PFAF. But its buzzer wasn't the only one on the console. I rang the third floor's, and we were promptly buzzed inside, no questions asked. Tiptoeing up the rickety wooden stairs, we listened for sounds. Fortunately, the third floor seemed totally uninterested in who might be visiting them and a sleepy hush prevailed in the building.

On the second floor, we found a door with a sticker slapped across it, announcing, "People For Animal Friends." This was the place!

After knocking and getting no answer, I took out my Swiss army knife and got to work picking Bettina's lock. A few moments later, the door sprang open, and Ned and I poked our heads in cautiously. Instead of an office, it was a messy living space. "Bettina's apartment!" I breathed, keeping my voice low in case she was asleep or showering. "Boy, did I guess wrong!"

On alert, we tiptoed around the apartment—a loft that included a kitchen and living area with a small adjoining bedroom. Fortunately, there was no sign of Bettina. "She's not here," I said, shooting Ned a relieved smile.

"But she could arrive home at any minute," he replied.

"So we need to search the place fast," I said, eyeing her cluttered desk with a sinking feeling. It would take hours to go through all this stuff. "Ned, would you mind checking out that file cabinet in the corner while I dig through Bettina's desk?"

"Why not?" Ned squeezed my shoulders affectionately before starting on his project.

A pile of animal magazines lay strewn across her gray metal desk, and I randomly picked up one called *Pet Peeves*. The main story, an interview with Bettina, featured a glossy picture of an unsmiling woman with intense eyes, her dark hair pulled back severely. Below the picture, the interviewer got to work asking her tough questions.

I quickly scanned the story, then crossed the room to join Ned. "Look at this," I said, setting down the magazine on top of the waist-high cabinet. "It's an interview with Bettina. First, the reporter asks, 'What are your feelings about using drastic measures like vandalism to get across your animal rights concerns?' Bettina replies, 'I've never supported that. I feel that organizations like mine should work within the law.'"

Ned read the next question. "'But what if activists

are unable to change the law?'" He raised his eyes to mine, frowning. "Bettina gives a weird answer to that question, don't you think, Nancy?"

"I sure do," I replied, reading out loud, 'I can understand why activists get frustrated and turn to more extreme measures if they can't change the laws they don't like.'"

Ned continued reading Bettina's quote. "'For instance, I've been working with the local town council to ban a coyote farm, Braeburn Farm, out-side River Heights, but so far I've seen no progress.'" Looking at me, he said, "Nancy, that must be the coy-ote farm Alicia gets her fur from."

"Must be. I mean, how many coyote farms does River Heights have?"

"I doubt there are many others around," Ned said. "I bet it's just some eccentric coyote guy who likes keeping them."

"Look at the next question, Ned," I said, focusing us back on the interview. "The reporter asks Bettina, 'What's wrong with a coyote farm?' and she answers, 'I don't believe in containing wild animals. They should roam free.'"

Ned glanced at the magazine, then back at me, his brown eyes troubled. "So what do you think, Nancy? Is this interview evidence Bettina might have vandal-ized Swoon 2?"

I frowned. "I don't know whether I'd call it evidence, but it does make me even more suspicious of her. Before I read the article, I couldn't figure out why Bettina had a problem with using the fur if the coyotes weren't harmed. But this interview makes it clear that she has a problem with fencing in wild animals. So maybe she vandalized the store because she thinks Alicia's business supports this evil farm."

A creak in the hallway outside interrupted our conversation. Quickly, we scanned the loft for a place to hide, but there were piles of clutter everywhere, including inside the closets and under the bed. Voices chattered outside the door, and I swept over to it, pressing my ear against it with Ned behind me. A woman's voice said, "Did you get your grocery delivery, darling?"

A man answered, "Whoops, I forgot to place the order online."

The woman said, "Well, someone rang our buzzer downstairs, and I assumed it was your groceries. I was in the bedroom on the phone when I buzzed them in. You were in the kitchen, so I just thought you'd taken care of it."

"No one came."

"How strange." Their voices trailed off as they descended the stairs. Phew! False alarm. No Bettina yet.

"Lucky us," Ned said, grinning. "So Nancy, what do you think? Are we done here? I'm worried that if Bettina comes home, there won't be any place to hide. She's such a packrat."

"You're right, Ned. Let's go. After reading that article, I think it might be worth a trip to Braeburn Farm to ask the owner if Bettina's been harassing him. I'm curious to know how aggressive she is about her animal campaigns. Do you want to come with me? Or do you have to get home?"

Ned checked his watch. "Six o'clock already. Wow. I told my parents I'd be home for dinner, but that won't be till eight since they had some early party to go to or something. So yeah, I'd love to come with you, Nancy."

"I guess we need directions there," I said, digging around Bettina's desk for a Rolodex. Luckily, I found one quickly, and it had a phone number for Braeburn Farm. As we headed outside to my car. I called the farm, which I discovered was in the country about a half hour outside of town.

"Why don't you just ask the guy about Bettina over the phone?" Ned asked after I'd hung up. "Save us a trip?"

"I thought of that, but he might think it was weird if I called him cold and started asking him nutty questions about animal activists harassing him," I said.

"Plus, I might find something at the farm that I'm not expecting. Some clue I wouldn't have found otherwise. Or not. But it's worth a try."

Ned ruffled my reddish-gold hair as I started the engine. "You're right, Nan. Because you never know—one thing can lead to another."

I shot him an affectionate grin. "That's what I'm counting on, Ned."

It was already dusk by the time we pulled into a long tree-lined driveway rimmed by empty pastures. Post-and-rail fences secured by wire enclosed the pastures, while a red sign with a brown coyote wearing glasses and tapping his forehead with a Grinch-like finger greeted us. The coyote was sitting cross-legged on the words, BRAEBURN FARM.

"Is that supposed to show how smart and wily coyotes are?" Ned wondered, rolling down his window to get a better look.

"The owner seems to like coyotes, even if he fences them in," I said.

"Maybe he's trying to protect them from hunters. He might see Bettina as cruel for wanting to free them into the dangerous wilderness." Ned's words were interrupted by the sudden appearance of a woman running. Tall and dark-haired, she blasted out of the nearby woods into the pasture next to us, a pack of coyotes on her trail, her waist-length ponytail whipping around her.

The coyotes made terrifying, high-pitched cackles as they bore down on her. Her eyes were wide with fright as she stumbled ten feet from the fence. In another moment, the coyotes would attack!

I screeched to a halt and jumped out of the car, clambering over the fence to help her before Ned could protest. Closing the ten feet between us in a split second, I clamped my hands under her shoulders and heaved her up. She struggled to her feet, getting ready to take off again, and then we froze, looking at the circle of wild yellow predatory eyes fencing us in.

7

Hidden Butterflies

"Ned, honk the horn!" I shouted.

The coyotes skittered at the sudden sound, but they didn't go far.

"Get!" Bettina shouted at them—I knew she was Bettina from the *Pet Peeves* photo. She waved her arms furiously at the coyotes, and I did the same. Since she was an animal person, I figured she knew what she was doing—sort of. I mean, she'd gotten herself into this situation, which didn't show the best judgment.

Still, waving our arms made the coyotes hesitate, and their yellow eyes went from killer to confused. "Get, get!" Bettina shrieked, while I clapped my hands loudly in between waves. Suddenly, bright blinding lights shone in our faces, and the coyotes froze, revealing a gap in their scattered circle. The fence beckoned from beyond.

Bettina grabbed my arm. "Don't run," she urged, "or they'll chase us. Back up slowly. Keep waving and shouting, though."

Slowly, carefully, I followed her lead, and we inched our way backward through the gap. Ned honked and flashed the headlights furiously, while Bettina and I kept up our waving and shouting routine. After a painfully long minute, my back hit pay dirt—the fence.

"Quick!" Bettina said. Her face next to me was as pale as the headlights. "Over the fence!"

I didn't need instructions. Before the coyotes could even think to chase us, I'd climbed up and over the fence in one lightning motion, with Bettina every bit as speedy at my side.

Ned jumped out of my car from the driver's side and rushed over to us. "Are you two okay?" he asked, gripping my shoulders. His face was as pale as Bettina's. "I can't believe what almost happened."

Bettina made a small hiccuping sound, and her brown eyes had a liquid shine to them, as if tears were about to spill over. Without warning, she flung her arms around Ned and exclaimed, "Thank you so much for saving us, whoever you are!"

"Whoa!" Ned said, looking a bit freaked as our gazes locked. "That's, uh, all right—any time."

"Bettina Quintana, I presume," I said, cutting in.

Now it was her turn to freak. She whipped around,

her eyes snapping fiercely. "How do you know me?" she asked suspiciously.

"I read your interview in *Pet Peeves*," I said. "I'm Nancy Drew, and this is my boyfriend, Ned Nickerson. We recognized you from your picture in the article. I'm surprised to see you here. I mean, since you don't like wild animals penned up, I would think it would upset you to see the coyotes like this." I was babbling, hoping she'd react and spill some information. "I'm just curious," I went on, "why were you in the pasture with them? Didn't you know they might chase you?"

She placed her hands on her hips. "Excuse me, Nancy or whatever your name is, is my business yours? I should be the one to ask what *you're* doing here?"

"The article in *Pet Peeves* made me sympathetic to your cause," I replied, fudging. "We found the idea of a coyote farm really strange, so we decided to come here and see for ourselves whether the coyotes are mistreated."

"Of course they are!" Bettina said hotly. "You don't have to see it to believe it. All you need to know is that wild animals are being confined and that's cruel."

A silver object glinting from the pocket of her jeans caught my eye. "Are those wire clippers?" I asked, pointing to them. "Were you planning to free the coyotes?"

Her eyes flashed fire. "Look, Nancy, I really appreciate that you saved me from the coyotes. Except they probably wouldn't have hurt me that badly when they realized I meant them no harm. But I don't need to stand here while you shoot questions at me that are none of your concern." She turned on her heel and began to jog down the driveway toward the main road.

"Wait!" I cried, sprinting to catch up. "Do you know Alicia Adams?"

Bettina stopped, looking at me with a face that seemed genuinely puzzled. "No," she said slowly. "Why?"

"Well then, do you know a store called Swoon 2?"

She shook her head. "Sorry Nancy. Now, can I go?"

"Please listen, Bettina," I pressed. "Because if you've never heard of Alicia or Swoon 2, you might be interested to know what happened today." I told her that Alicia, the owner of Swoon, had discovered the anti-cruelty slogans on the wall when she opened the store this morning. Then I mentioned the notes in the coyote fur jackets that PFAF had supposedly signed. "The customers freaked when they found those notes," I said.

"Awesome!" Bettina said, looking impressed. "I wish I could say I was responsible, because any clothes made with coyote fur should be banned on principle. Even if the coyotes weren't harmed, most people who see the jackets don't realize that. It sends the wrong message."

Ned, who had caught up to us a few seconds ago, asked, "But do you really believe that vandalizing places sends the right message?"

Bettina shrugged. "Honestly, several months ago I would have agreed that breaking in like that would be too extreme, but recently I've changed my mind. Getting animal rights laws passed in this town has been a nightmare. People just don't take animals that seriously, and I'm frustrated by how slow everything is. The town council goes on vacation while laws wait to be passed, or there's stuff they think is more important." She threw up her hands. "Meanwhile, the coyotes are suffering at this ridiculous farm."

"But what if they're safe here?" I asked, hoping to provoke her into spilling more information. "They might get hurt by predators in the wild. Also, they might kill animals you'd like to protect, like raccoons and groundhogs."

"Coyotes don't have many predators," Bettina said, "only wolves, and there aren't any around here. Plus, coyotes keep the natural order in place by not allowing too many small animals to take over. They keep things balanced."

"But aren't there plenty of other coyotes for that?" Ned asked.

"I'm concerned about these coyotes and keeping them out of prison! Their lives are awful here—it's downright abusive." While she was speaking, I sneaked a look at her ears. No butterfly earrings there, but that didn't mean she hadn't taken them. Bettina added, "If I can say anything about myself, it's that I'm honest. I had nothing to do with the vandalism at that store." Her eyes gleamed fervently. "If only I had done it!"

"Look Bettina," I said, "I understand you feel strongly about the coyotes, but tampering with other people's things is against the law. So you'd better leave the coyotes alone. If they disappear, Ned and I will be witnesses to your being here with wire cutters in your pocket."

"But I haven't cut anything yet," she protested. "I was just trying to get an idea of what their enclosure was like before taking action. Speaking of which, I've had enough action for the evening. I've got to get back to my car before a cop sees it and traces me to the farm. If I'm caught, this won't be the first time Braeburn's owner accuses me of stalking and trespassing. Which is *so* not the case," she added quickly. "By the way, could you give me a ride to my car? It's along the main road. I just don't want anyone to see me."

I shrugged. "Sure, hop in."

A few minutes later, Ned and I dropped Bettina off at her car, which was parked in a hidden nook off the road. All her resentment toward me and my nosy questions seemed to have vanished, and she thanked me heartily for the two minute ride.

"So what do you make of Bettina, Nancy?" Ned asked me on our way back to River Heights.

"I think she's not as straightforward as she believes she is," I said. "She claims she's honest, but I think she'd lie if that would help her agenda. The funny thing is, I was telling her the truth when I said I was sympathetic to her cause—you know that. I totally think animal rights are important, but I don't agree with her that vandalism is okay."

"Do you think she really wasn't responsible for the vandalism?"

I was silent for a moment, considering Bettina's reaction to the news of the notes and scrawls. "You know, Ned," I said, "she seemed so surprised when we told her about the stuff at the store, and I don't think she's that good an actress. So yes, even though I don't think she'd hesitate to lie when she needs to, I think she's for real when she claims she's not the vandal. Your thoughts?"

"The same. But then, who wrote all that stuff—and why?"

I sighed. "It could be anybody. Someone who wants to hurt Alicia and blame PFAF. I haven't totally written off Bettina, but I'm guessing our energy is better spent chasing other suspects."

"Like Mr. Tsao," Ned said.

"Maybe," I replied, wishing I had more leads.

On the edge of town, Ned answered a cell call from his dad, who told him that he and Ned's mom wouldn't be home for dinner because their party was lasting longer than expected. Ned's father is the editor of the *River Heights Bugle,* so his parents get invited out a lot to social and civic events.

Ned said, "Since I'm not eating with Mom and Dad tonight, how about we grab a sandwich and stop in at *Threads*? I'd like to lay out some photos I took of models wearing Alicia's designs. We did a whole photo shoot the day before her opening. The pictures are supposed to go with an article about Alicia in next month's issue." He glanced at me as we drove down River Street, where the *Threads* offices were located. "I could use your help, Nan, if you have time."

"You've got it, Ned," I replied, smiling. "For one thing, I'd like to see what you've been doing all these weeks."

But once we were upstairs in the glossy *Threads* offices, I had mixed feelings about agreeing to help Ned with this project. As I laid out photos on his computer, I couldn't help feeling a pang at the sight of these gorgeous women my boyfriend spent his days photographing.

"I'll never believe you again when you claim this is work, Ned," I teased, scanning a picture of a model with coffee-colored skin and high cheekbones into the computer. She wore a black and pink leotard with a lush pink skirt that resembled a tutu, slightly longer than the kind ballerinas wear. Her gold hoop earrings were half the size of her face, and she struck a sort of haughty pose with her feet apart and hands on her hips. The effect was glamorous, a bit scary, and very cool. "You've got to admit, Ned, these models are pretty awesome-looking," I added.

"Yeah, well, if you want to know the truth, Nancy, I'd much rather help you with your mysteries than take pictures of these women. Models can be so into their appearances, and that subject gets old after, say, the first minute. I'm sure these models couldn't think their way out of a circle of lunging coyotes nearly as well as you did," Ned added cheerfully.

I laughed. "Thanks, Ned. Now I know I have a special talent."

"You never know when it'll come in handy," Ned joked, squeezing my shoulders. He checked his watch and added, "Hey, it's nine thirty already. Later than I thought. I'm actually sort of tired. Maybe I'll finish this work at home tomorrow."

"Helping me sneak into lofts and wrangle coyotes and deal with Bettina—that's so not tiring," I said wryly. "But seriously, Ned, how are you going to transfer your files from your computer here to your laptop at home? Do you have a thumb drive you can use to back them up?"

Rummaging in his desk, Ned said, "There's one around here somewhere. Or maybe not. Anyway, there's definitely one in Natalie's supply closet. You know, Natalie Stephanoff, the alpha reporter?"

"Deirdre's boss," I said, remembering the small, intense woman who was covering Alicia's sale for *Threads*. "Why don't I check out her supply closet for a thumb drive while you pack up?"

"Great, Nancy. Thanks. Natalie's office is two doors down on the right."

I scooted out the door to prowl Natalie's office. Helping Ned with his work was the least I could do after he's been such a dedicated assistant sleuth.

In the hall, I stopped short. Natalie's office light was on. It was Saturday night. How weird was that? But maybe Natalie was just as hard-working as Ned was.

I peeked into the office, then reeled back as if I'd been jerked. The woman inside the office wasn't Natalie. No way. She was a taller, thinner brunette by the name of Deirdre Shannon!

For a moment, I watched Deirdre poke around the

office and open a desk drawer. With a puzzled frown, Deirdre reached into the drawer and drew out a pair of earrings. Their translucent blue stones gleamed in the office's bright overhead glare, butterfly wings sparkling.

Then she turned—and saw me.

8

Trapped

W hat are *you* doing here?" we asked at the same time.

I explained first. "I'm helping Ned lay out some photos he took of models wearing Alicia's designs. He needs a thumb drive to back up his files, and I'm told there's a supply cabinet in this office where I can find one. Now it's your turn, Deirdre. What are *you* doing here?"

She frowned. "If Ned's getting help from you, that means he shouldn't take credit for the magazine spread. It's, like, not his work."

"Deirdre, it *is* his work. He shot the pictures. He's making the decisions about lay out, which will be checked out by his boss anyway. I'm just helping him do grunt work like scanning photos onto his computer. But we're getting off topic here. You've haven't answered my question. I've caught you red-handed in your boss's drawer."

Her eyes shifted away from mine. "I'm looking for a notepad. My old one is already filled with notes for articles. That's how hard I've been working."

"Did you know that a pair of earrings just like the ones you're holding are missing from Swoon 2?" I said.

Deirdre dropped the earrings back in the drawer as if they were red hot. "I don't know what you're talking about, Nancy!" she huffed. "*I* didn't take the earrings from Swoon 2. I just found this pair in Natalie's drawer while I was looking for supplies. I held them up because I thought they were pretty. I never intended to take them, and you have no evidence to support your accusation!"

"I never accused you of stealing earrings, Deirdre," I said, "from Alicia or Natalie. I only asked whether you knew they'd gone missing from Swoon 2. Do you know why they've turned up in Natalie's drawer?"

"None of your business. This is between Natalie and me."

"Well, does Natalie know you're snooping in her

desk, Deirdre? I mean, if you really wanted a notepad, you'd be searching the supply cabinet, not your boss's desk."

The scalding expression in Deirdre's eyes could have fried an egg. "Don't you dare tell Natalie you found me here, Nancy! You won't, will you?"

"I don't mind keeping your secret, but you still haven't answered my question. Tell me the truth, not some lame excuse."

Deirdre sighed, and the fire went out of her eyes—for now. "Yes, I heard about the vandalism at Swoon 2. Who hasn't by now? And I heard about the missing earrings, too. And you know what, Nancy?" she added, her eyes snapping again. "I want to solve this case myself. I can do a much better job than you. In fact, I'm assuming you're investigating for Alicia, but I'm investigating for myself because I'm curious to know who trashed the store and why. It'll be a race between you and me to see who finds the guilty person first."

"Do you suspect Natalie?" I asked.

"That's info I'm keeping to myself! Why should I share it with my competition?"

I rolled my eyes. "Fine. I'll see you around, Deirdre." A standing closet built into the wall near the door caught my eye. The supply cabinet, probably.

I grabbed a thumb drive from a box inside it and returned to Ned.

He also rolled his eyes when I told him about my encounter with Deirdre. "You'd think she'd get over this competition stuff," Ned said. "If she really cares about Alicia, wouldn't she just want to get the case solved ASAP so Alicia can get some sleep at night?"

I shrugged. "It's not exactly Deirdre's style to care about Alicia. She cares about glory for herself, and being the first person to solve this case would get her that." As we'd been speaking, Ned had been sitting in front of his computer, clicking occasionally on pictures he wanted to enlarge. He clicked on a new one, and I did a double take. The model in the picture wore a sweeping turquoise and chartreuse satin gown—and the butterfly earrings!

"Ned, look!" I cried, pointing. "How coincidental is that?"

Ned clicked on the earrings to enlarge them. As far as I could tell, they were identical to the ones in Natalie's drawer, though I admit I only snatched a quick look at those from several feet away.

"When were these pictures taken?" I asked.

"Thursday. The day before the opening," Ned told me.

"Maybe Alicia lent the earrings to Natalie for the

photo shoot along with the clothes and just forgot she'd done that," I said. "But why would Natalie keep the earrings in an unlocked drawer when the shoot has been over for a couple days?"

Ned shrugged. "I can't even guess." He turned his attention back to the computer. "Thanks for the thumb drive, Nancy. I'll just transfer my files and shut down."

On the way to the elevator bank, we passed Natalie's office. Deirdre was still inside, holding court in Natalie's chair. She took a moment from her note jotting to throw us a scowl. "If Deirdre wasn't still there," I murmured to Ned as we waited for an elevator, "I'd search the office myself. Deirdre obviously suspects Natalie, and I'm curious to know why."

"The earrings, probably," Ned said.

"Yes, but what made Deirdre search the office in the first place?" I paused, then added, "Is it Natalie's responsibility to return the clothes and jewelry? Because if it is, Deirdre might have wondered why the earrings didn't get to Alicia."

Ned frowned. "I think it *is* Natalie's responsibility, actually."

"I'll just have to move faster on this case, because Deirdre is willing to lose sleep to solve it first. And if she does, River Heights will never hear the end of it!"

•   •   •

Sunday, over lunch at the Moonbeam Diner, I summed up the case for Bess and George. Ned was working at home on his photo layout, but my best friends had joined me. "I have two and a half suspects so far," I told them. "Bettina is only half a suspect because she really sounded believable when she denied knowing about the vandalism. My lie detector radar is usually right."

"I bet Bettina would have been proud to claim the vandalism if she'd done it," George said.

"But how do you explain the PFAF notes in the pockets?" Bess asked. "And the scrawls?"

"Maybe the guilty person is trying to shift suspicion from themselves by blaming Bettina," I said. "Which brings me to my next two suspects, Mr. Tsao and Natalie."

"Well, the missing earrings are in Natalie's possession—not a good sign," George said. "Also, Deirdre found other reasons to suspect Natalie, or she wouldn't have been snooping in the first place."

"Fat chance getting Deirdre to tell us her reasons," Bess said. "As for Mr. Tsao, how do we explain the sequins on his floor and his card at the crime scene?"

"He's the most likely suspect, don't you think, Nancy?" George asked.

I had to agree. My next stop that afternoon would be Mr. Tsao's office. Unfortunately, Bess and George had both promised to babysit siblings, so I was on my own.

After lunch, I went home briefly to ask Dad for Mr. Tsao's address. "Be careful, Nancy," Dad warned as he wrote it down for me. "He's not likely to be there on Sunday, but you never know. He's not someone you want to tangle with."

"Thanks, Dad, but don't worry about me. I'll be fine."

Five minutes later, I was following Dad's meticulous directions, which happened to lead me down River Street and past Swoon 2. A shadow passed inside the store window, reminding me that it was open for business on Sundays. It wouldn't hurt to ask Alicia a few questions before moving on to the offices of Michael Tsao, Esq. I parked the car.

Once inside, I found Alicia and an assistant helping customers. Alicia looked up at me with a bright smile. "No further incidents of vandalism or theft," she announced when her customers were busy elsewhere. "That's progress!"

"About those butterfly earrings," I said. "I found them in Natalie Stephanoff's desk drawer. Did you lend them to her for the photo shoot?"

Alicia nodded. "I had two pairs of those earrings in my inventory here. They've proved popular at my Chicago store, so I decided to carry more than one pair here. Anyway, Thursday, the day before my opening, I lent several outfits plus jewelry to *Threads*. The *Threads* stylist returned all the clothes Thursday evening, but the jewelry had been put in a safe deposit box at the bank for safekeeping earlier that day. Since the bank was closed Thursday night, the stylist promised she'd get the jewelry to me on Friday. Then Friday was such a zoo, and the store had to close, so she promised to return it tomorrow when the bank reopens. But now you're telling me the earrings aren't at the bank—they're in Natalie Stephanoff's drawer?"

"One pair is," I said. "I guess there's no way to know which pair Natalie is hiding—the stolen one or the borrowed one."

Alicia's face clouded. "So do you think Natalie might have stolen them, Nancy? Do you think *she* could have vandalized this place?"

I was silent for a moment, then asked, "Alicia, do you know any reason why Natalie might have a grudge against you?"

"Why should she have a grudge against me?" Alicia asked, looking a bit freaked. "I barely know her.

In fact, she was sweet to feature my designs in the next issue of *Threads*."

"Well, can you think of anyone else who might have something against you? I mean, besides Michael Tsao and PFAF?"

Alicia frowned. "That's sort of a troubling question to answer. I'm a pretty easy-going person, and to think that some creep might have it in for me—that's just unsettling." She paused, her brow puckered in thought. "You know, there is someone else, actually. Jean-Georges."

"Jean-Georges? Who's he?"

"Jean-Georges de Vouvray. He's an old boyfriend of mine from my modeling days in Paris," Alicia explained.

"But how much of a threat could he be to you from France?" I asked. "Unless, of course, he's visiting here."

"He's more than a visitor," Alicia said. "He's a U.S. resident with a permanent green card. See, Jean-Georges married a woman named Campbell Harris, who happened to be my roommate in Paris. She's a rich Chicago heiress. That's where they live now."

"Wow!" I exclaimed, intrigued. "So did you introduce Campbell to Jean-Georges way back when?"

"Yes, but that's not why there's bad stuff between

Jeans-Georges and me," Alicia said. "After a year or so of going out, I realized I wasn't all that in love with him. He started seeing Campbell after we broke up. I was fine with that."

"So . . . why the grudge? Was his ego hurt when you ended the relationship?"

"No, it was nothing like that, Nancy. Nothing romantic. Our problem is business related. See, Jean-Georges is a fashion designer, and ever since he moved here with Campbell, he's been trying to establish his label in the American market, especially the Chicago area."

"Without much success?" I asked.

"Oh, he's had some success. Most young designers would be thrilled with the business he's been doing. It's just that I've been doing better. There are so many women who love the Swoon label. They're completely devoted to my designs. And Jean-Georges is frustrated that he can't seem to shake out a share of my market for himself." Even though Alicia was complimenting her own designs, she spoke without any kind of arrogance about them. She was simply telling me the facts.

"So he's angry at you because he can't take the competition?" I asked. "Isn't that a bit extreme?"

"If it was just a matter of me winning more customers, he'd be okay—not happy with the situation, but not full of revenge either," Alicia explained. "No, Jean-Georges is convinced that I ripped off some of his ideas from the old days when we dated and brain-stormed together. He believes my success is owed to designs I allegedly stole from him."

"Why does he think you stole them?" I asked.

"Because some of his designs resemble mine, but he made them later."

"That doesn't make sense," I said. "It would be more reasonable for you to think he ripped you off."

"Except that he never saw my earlier designs." Alicia brightened. "Hey, Nancy. Are you busy tomorrow night? Because if you're not, you could meet Jean-Georges at the Fashion Awards Dinner. Jean-Georges and I and a few other designers are up for awards. It's going to be held at the Belmont Hotel in Chicago. Would you like to come along as my date? Maybe you could get a chance to talk to him—sneak in a few questions."

"Your date, Alicia?" I said, and grinned. "Sure! I mean, I doubt Ned will have a problem with that."

Alicia laughed. "Now, there's always the danger that Jean-Georges won't speak to anyone who's a friend of mine. So once we're at the dinner, we won't make it obvious we know each other. But I'll lobby behind the scenes for you and Jean-Georges to be seated next to each other."

"Great. I'll see you there tomorrow! Meanwhile, I'll call the Belmont Hotel to reserve a room for myself."

"By the way," Alicia said, "the event starts at seven. It includes a fashion show with a sampling of the nominees' collections. And many thanks for all your help. I really appreciate it."

After saying good-bye to Alicia, I headed outside and made a quick cell phone call to get reservations at the Belmont Hotel. My brain was swirling with thoughts of a new lead, Jean-Georges de Vouvray. True, there wasn't enough evidence against him to call him a suspect yet. There was only Alicia's hunch that he had it in for her. But I was frustrated by my lack of progress with my other suspects, and even if Jean-Georges didn't pan out, I could look forward to a glittery fashion dinner in Chicago.

Still, I shouldn't lose sight of Mr. Tsao. Of all my suspects, he made the most sense—if only I could figure out why he'd be blaming animal rights activists. Maybe my investigation this afternoon would shed some light.

Mr. Tsao's office was only three blocks away from Swoon 2—a three minute walk. Once in the lobby of his building, I explained to the guard that I was working overtime for Mr. Tsao. He didn't question me; in fact, his droopy eyes told me he was barely awake.

I pressed the elevator Up button, and while waiting, I scanned the register of tenants and found Michael Tsao, Esq. on the tenth floor along with Finch & Sullivan, Attorneys-at-Law. Soon, the door to the nearest elevator slid open, and I stepped in eagerly. While Mr. Tsao's office would surely be locked, maybe I could talk my way in. Maybe the guard had a master key to the offices in the building. First things first, though. It made sense to ride up and scope out the situation before approaching him.

Just as the elevator door was closing, a man slipped through it. I did a double take. It was Mr. Tsao! A stocky man with deep frown lines, he looked a bit older than his image in his photos. He made no eye contact with me, so I stared at the floor indicator above the door. My spirits rose. Who knew? Meeting Mr. Tsao in person might be a lucky break. Maybe I could convince him I worked for Finch & Sullivan and needed to borrow supplies.

The elevator lurched upward, and the first floor indicator light was no longer glowing red. Suddenly, before the light shifted to the second floor, the elevator jolted to a stop. After a few seconds, the door still didn't open. Were we stuck? Unless I was very much mistaken, I'd have more to talk about with Mr. Tsao than just the events at Swoon 2!

9

Teen Model

Mr. Tsao jabbed his finger into the tenth floor button. Nothing happened. The elevator wouldn't budge, and no matter how many buttons he jabbed—harder each time—the panel stayed dark. Above us, the floor indicator revealed no info about where we were. Obviously, we'd been sucked into some strange void, like the Bermuda triangle of elevator shafts.

With the Door Open button as his next victim, Mr. Tsao punched it with a finger that by this time was so shaky he barely made contact. I pushed also, but to no avail. Great! We were stuck.

Mr. Tsao still wouldn't look at me, but I could tell he didn't know who I was. If he had recognized me, he would have acknowledged my existence.

The vibe I got was major annoyance that such an inconvenience should befall someone as important as he was.

"Let's press the alarm," I suggested, leaning across him to hit the red button. It didn't sound, or anyway, we couldn't hear it.

"Help!" Mr. Tsao shouted through the tiny crack between the door and the elevator floor. "Hey you, guard!"

I took up his cry. "We're stuck! Can you hear us?"

"The lazy fool is asleep!" Mr. Tsao spat.

"It's hard to believe he can't hear the alarm," I said.

"Maybe he's ignoring us on purpose," Mr. Tsao said bitterly. "He never liked me. I make lots of demands, and he'd rather sit and do nothing."

Mr. Tsao definitely seemed the demanding type. If I were a guard, I'd resent someone as bossy as Mr. Tsao. Still, I couldn't believe the guard would ignore two stuck people because he didn't like one of them.

"The overhead lights are still on," I observed. "That means the electricity still functions in the building."

"Maybe a fuse blew," Mr. Tsao said. "Something that governs the elevator controls but not the overhead lights." He sighed heavily. "Now what?"

"I wish my friend Bess were here," I said. "She's

mechanically gifted. She could get us out of this fix."

"Wishing isn't going to get us out of this box, young lady!" Mr. Tsao snapped. "Next time, say something helpful."

"You might try being nicer to the person you're stuck with," I suggested. "Just an idea. I mean, you have no idea how long we'll be in this thing together."

A thunderlike scowl raged across Mr. Tsao's face. "How dare you speak to me like that? I'm nice to people when I choose to be—people who earn my respect. That takes time. So far, you haven't passed my test."

I bit my lip, hoping his anger would make him careless and he'd spill some juicy info.

"The building maintenance here is laughable," he went on wrathfully. "Is this the kind of service my rent dollars are buying? A stuck elevator when I want to get paperwork done on a Sunday afternoon? I'm going to move my office away from this rathole the moment I find a new space, and if I don't get my security deposit back, I'll sue the idiot landlord. He's going to hear from me the moment I bust out of here. Okay, so it's Sunday, but I'll track him down!"

Mr. Tsao continued his rant for a few more minutes. Then he grew quiet as worry replaced anger as his top emotion. Whipping out a cell phone, he attempted to punch numbers, but his fingers were even shakier than before.

"Let me try mine," I said.

"You won't have any success," he said gloomily. "We're in a dead zone here. I was just hoping my phone would decide to work this time."

My own cell told me he was right. Absolutely no service. But actually, that was okay with me. I'd just put this bad situation to good use. We were in this metal box together, and no matter how hard he tried, he wouldn't be able to weasel out of my questions.

Fudging, I said, "This stuck elevator has wrecked my day. See, I'm a paralegal at Finch & Sullivan, and I was hoping to finish up some work that landed on my desk late Friday afternoon."

I sneaked a glance at him to see whether he cared. He cocked his head at me, looking sort of interested. Feeling encouraged, I went on, "The case involves that poor woman, Alicia Adams. She has to defend herself against all these ridiculous lawsuits thanks to this mob scene at her store on Friday. But it wasn't her fault people got hurt."

Mr. Tsao's face turned crimson. Could his bottled-up anger possibly rocket the elevator upward? "You don't know what you're talking about!" he exploded. "My daughter was injured on Alicia Adams's premises. She deserves recompense, for her hospital costs *and* for her emotional distress. Haven't you learned anything about the law?"

"I know about the law. I'm a paralegal."

"Obviously not a very good one!" he cried. "The law states that the property owner is responsible for injuries on site. That's the law." He finished his tirade by punching the wall.

The lights flickered, the elevator shook, and then— silence. Mr. Tsao's face paled. I took advantage of the quiet. "Did you know that Swoon 2 was vandalized after everyone went home Friday night?"

"How would I know that?" he replied. "I've never set foot in the store in my life."

"Not even to find out information for your lawsuit?"

"Oh, I plan to visit the store in good time," he said. "Meanwhile, my daughter's injuries have absorbed all of my attention."

"I'm sorry about her injuries." Like Bettina, Mr. Tsao seemed genuinely surprised to learn about the vandalism. But I wanted to make sure.

Mr. Tsao smirked, as if he had a sudden happy thought. "What kind of vandalism are you talking about, anyway?" he asked. I told him about the ripped dress, the graffiti and notes, and the missing earrings, then finished by saying, "Your business card was found on the floor, under a rack of clothes." I took it out of my pocket and showed it to him. "But you really claim you've never been there?"

He peered at the card, then took it from my hand and put it in his pocket. "That card's mine, all right. Barbara must have dropped it in all the pandemonium. I'd given her my card a few days ago for a friend of hers who needs legal advice."

I wanted to ask about the sequins, but I didn't want to disclose that I'd been in his house. "Well, I hope Barbara won't be angry at Alicia for long. I'm sure Barbara would like to own some of those designs eventually—the Swoon dresses with sequins are especially beautiful."

"Barbara already has plenty of dresses with sequins," he said. "She wore one the other night to some party or other. I don't know why she'd need to buy more. Especially from that woman!"

Hmm. So the sequins on Mr. Tsao's carpet could have come from something Barbara already owned. My mind clicked to our present circumstances, and I checked my watch. We'd been here about fifteen minutes, and the elevator was starting to get hot. No cell phone service, no alarm, no guard. I'm usually patient, but even I was beginning to get frustrated.

I mean, did I really want to spend any more of my Sunday afternoon locked up with Mr. Tsao?

I jabbed the Door Open button hard three times. Mr. Tsao must have been reading my mind, because at the same moment he punched the elevator again. As if we were some coordinated magic act, the door lurched open, leaving a three foot gap between the elevator floor and the top of the lobby door. I blinked in amazement. A miracle! We could slither out, as long as we were careful not to fall backward into the open shaft behind us. I explained my thoughts to Mr. Tsao.

He replied, "Yes, but the elevator could suddenly move while we're halfway out of this thing and then we'd be crushed. It's not a way I want to die."

"Me neither, but I also don't want to spend all night in here. Why don't I go first? Then, if you don't feel like following me, at least I can go for help."

He frowned, considering. "Okay, young lady, you first."

I took a deep breath, crouched down, and crawled through the narrow opening. The white marble of the lobby floor sparkled about six feet below me. Not too bad a jump, as long as I took care not to lose my balance backward. Who knew how deep the shaft behind me was? Sure, I didn't want to spend the night in the elevator with Mr. Tsao, but I'd be even less thrilled in the subbasement with the elevator dangling above me.

"Go on!" Mr. Tsao snarled, not like a cheerleader, but more like an irritated boss. I couldn't wait to leap. And as soon as I did—an easy jump—I shot a look at the guard, who was snoring lightly as he rested his head on the front desk. I glanced back through the space at Mr. Tsao. "Look, either you can follow me, or I can wake the guard and get him to help you."

"No, no, I'll jump," Mr. Tsao said. "If I've said it once, I've said it a thousand times—the man's a fool."

Once Mr. Tsao had landed safely, he stormed to the front desk and shook the guard awake just as I pushed through the revolving doors to the sidewalk outside, free at last.

I fingered my car keys in my jeans' pocket. Time to go to Ned's and see how he was coming with his work.

Ned greeted me at his front door, and I wasted no time telling him about my episode with Mr. Tsao. He said, "Sounds like you could use a soda, Nancy. Come into the kitchen and let's grab a can from the fridge."

Soon, Ned and I were sitting in his computer room, drinking sodas and looking at his work for *Threads* on the monitor. "So, how are things?" I asked.

"Almost done. I just have to make a few adjustments." As Ned studied his final layout, I caught a glimpse of an issue of *Flair* he was using for inspiration. Not that I'm a fashion hound or anything, but I was curious to check out styles I might be seeing at the show tomorrow in Chicago.

But as I flipped through the magazine, I realized it was ten years old. Some of the pages were striking. One four-page spread featured a blue-eyed model whose long blond hair swept over brightly colored chiffon dresses and silk pants. The clothes sort of reminded me of outfits you'd see in movies taking place in the sixties—Alicia's style. A retro look, even for ten years ago. Orange, yellow, and pink were the main colors, but lime green was a favorite, too. "Alicia's stuff hasn't changed that much," I said, musing to myself as I flipped through the spread. And that was true. The designs were colorful, zesty, and creative rather than tailored and subdued.

Ned peeked over my shoulder. "Actually, those clothes aren't Alicia's. Look again."

I scanned the small print for the designer's name. "Jean-Georges de Vouvray?" His name popped out at me like neon. How could I have taken so long to see it? "Alicia's old boyfriend!" I exclaimed.

"Really?" Ned said, pushing back a lock of his

brown hair as he looked down at the page. "I don't blame you for thinking the designer was Alicia. Their stuff is so much alike."

I filled Ned in on the conversation I'd had with Alicia earlier. The time with Mr. Tsao had temporarily wiped Alicia's info from my brain. "I hate to admit this, Ned, but I don't blame Jean-Georges for feeling ripped off," I said. "Alicia's designs are so much like his. *I* know she didn't steal his designs because she told me she'd made them earlier, but he doesn't know that."

"While I was checking out magazines, I thought the same thing," Ned declared. "I was amazed by how similar their designs are. That's why I decided to use this spread—to see how designs like Alicia's were handled."

I studied the first page of the spread. A blurb at the bottom shouted, "Family Affair!" The text went on to explain that the model's name was Campbell Harris, and that she was engaged to the clothing designer himself.

"I wonder why Alicia never set Jean-Georges straight about her designs," Ned said.

I shrugged. "Maybe she just didn't feel like talking to him anymore. Tomorrow, I can question both Alicia and Jean-Georges. At separate times, of course." I told Ned about the Fashion Awards Dinner. "I'd like to get a head start on Jean-Georges by checking out his pad."

"Nancy, that doesn't sound like a good idea," Ned said, frowning. Like Dad, he often worried about my safety. And, like Dad, I always reassured him.

"Ned, I'll be careful. Fashion designers don't sound all that dangerous, anyway, though I guess he could threaten me with his graffiti pen."

"Or scissors," Ned said gravely. "Don't forget about the shredded dress!"

"I won't," I said, smirking. "But there's nothing wrong with me going up to Chicago tomorrow morning to do some snooping before the big night. Since Jean-Georges is a new lead, I might as well spend the whole day checking him out before I meet him at the dinner. Maybe he has a store or a work-shop." I brightened. "Maybe I'll see if Bess wants to go with me."

Not long after Ned and I said good night, I was sitting at our dining room table with Dad and Hannah, eating Hannah's home-cooked pot roast and looking forward to her awesome chocolate cake. Just as I was about to take my last bite of pot roast, the phone rang.

I answered it in the kitchen. Bess's voice greeted me through the receiver. "Nancy, guess what!" she said, so excited she could barely get her words out. "Alicia just asked me to model her clothes at the Fashion Awards Dinner tomorrow night. Hundreds of people will be watching. I am so petrified. Help!"

10

A Stormy Sail

B ess, how cool is that?" I cried.

"No, it's *terrifying.*" But Bess's ecstatic voice betrayed her true thoughts.

"Bess, you'll be awesome, I promise. How did you luck out like this?"

"Well, the model who had been assigned to wear Alicia's designs came down with the flu at the last minute," Bess explained. "For some reason, Alicia thought I'd look okay in her clothes, so she called to sign me on."

"For some reason?" I echoed. "Bess, you're way too modest. It's obvious she thought you'd be the best person to show off her clothes to the judges. But you know what, Bess? I'm planning a trip to Chicago tomorrow, too." I told Bess the whole scoop, from learning about Jean-Georges, to Alicia inviting me to the dinner, to my decision to drive to Chicago early to investigate Jean-Georges. "So, Bess," I continued, "here's the bottom line. I was going to call you anyway after dinner, because I think you'd be the perfect companion for my trip. How about leaving a few hours earlier than you'd planned and helping me scope out Jean-Georges? If you go to bed early enough tonight, you'll still get your beauty sleep."

Bess giggled. "Okay, Nancy, if I look pale and sleep deprived on the runway tomorrow evening, it'll be your fault. But seriously, I'd love to come. You know I can't resist helping you with a mystery. Also, if Jean-Georges has a showroom, he probably has some cool clothes there for sale. Count me in!"

Bess and I hung up and I returned to the table, where Dad and Hannah were already halfway through their cake. Hannah said, "Nancy, I saved your last bite of roast—it's on the kitchen counter—but if you're ready to move on to cake, then be my guest."

"Thanks, Hannah." I swung into the kitchen, finished off the pot roast, then cut myself a piece of cake. Even though I love Hannah's food, I couldn't wrap my mind around anything but Bess's news. Returning to the table with a slice of rich chocolate cake with creamy fudge icing, I apologized to Dad and Hannah. "I shouldn't have talked for so long during dinner," I said. "I guess this mystery has been making me forget basic things, like food and family." I told Dad and Hannah about Bess modeling for Alicia, and our early road trip to Chicago the next morning. "So Jean-Georges is a new lead, though Mr. Tsao is still a possibility," I added.

"I'm glad you're done investigating Michael Tsao for now, Nancy," Dad said, "but do be careful with this new guy, Jean-Georges."

"Yes, Nancy," Hannah seconded. "I'm glad Bess will be there with you."

The next morning, Bess and I set out for Chicago, armed with Jean-Georges's address. I'd called Alicia first thing to get it, and Bess was happy to learn that Jean-Georges's home address included a showroom for his designs.

As Bess and I zoomed up the interstate, we talked about the case so far. "I've sort of ruled out Bettina and Mr. Tsao," I said. "There was nothing in Bettina's house that connected her with the vandalism. Of course, the place was such a mess, I couldn't check out everything. Still, I think she would have admitted her guilt."

"But I don't get why you're discounting Mr. Tsao," Bess said. "You found those sequins on his bedroom floor and his business card at the scene of the crime, plus he has a motive for wanting to make Alicia's life miserable."

"The sequins could have fallen off one of his daughter's dresses," I explained. "Maybe she went into his bedroom to look for something. There was a full length mirror there, I remember, and maybe she doesn't have one in her room. As for the card, Mr. Tsao claimed that Barbara had taken it. It might have dropped out of her pocket or something when she was pushed into the window. It's true Mr. Tsao wants to make Alicia's life miserable, but he has plenty of legal ways to do that. He doesn't need to become a vandal."

"But those notes from PFAF," Bess said. "I mean, I don't think you should write off Bettina so quickly."

"Maybe not, but I have a sixth sense for suspects who are lying to me. Those two just aren't hitting my radar. Which brings me to Natalie and Jean-Georges."

"That whole episode with Deirdre is so weird, Nancy," Bess said, shaking her head in disgust. "I can't believe she snooped in her boss's drawer and then expected you to keep her secret!"

"I'm not surprised by her behavior at all, to tell you the truth. It's so typical of her to feel entitled like that. But you're right—Deirdre was totally out of line." After a pause, I added, "Do me a favor, Bess.

Call Alicia. She's probably on her way to Chicago, too, but her cell number is with the directions she gave us. Ask her whether she got the jewelry back from *Threads* and whether the butterfly earrings are there. The bank is open by now, so maybe the stylist was able to return the jewelry. You can use my cell phone—it's in my purse."

"No problem, Nancy," Bess said cheerfully. A quick cell phone call told us that the jewelry, minus the butterfly earrings, came safely back to Swoon 2 shortly before Alicia left the store ten minutes ago. So now Alicia was missing both pairs of earrings, though at least she knew one pair was in Natalie's drawer.

"So the earrings Natalie stashed must be the ones on loan to *Threads*, not the pair taken from the store," I mused.

Bess frowned. "How do you figure that, Nancy?"

"Because if a pair of butterfly earrings had come back from the bank, that would mean the pair in Natalie's drawer were the stolen ones. But since the earrings haven't come back, that means Natalie must have taken them from the stash at some point and put them in her drawer."

"In other words, she stole *that* pair," Bess said flatly.

"Maybe, but I bet she just borrowed them and

forgot to tell Alicia. I mean, it would be pretty obvious if the earrings, which had been seen by everyone at *Threads*, suddenly disappeared from the rest of the jewelry stash."

"Still, why is she hiding them?" Bess asked. "Why those earrings? Ones that match the stolen pair?"

"Good questions, Bess," I said. "If I don't nab Jean-Georges today, Natalie is first on my list to investigate tomorrow."

After another hour or so, Bess and I found ourselves on the outskirts of Chicago. She began reading me Alicia's directions, and after a series of exits and turns, we found Jean-Georges's building. "Not bad!" Bess exclaimed, as we stared up at the opulent nineteenth-century factory building converted into luxury lofts. "Looks like a palace." The sculpted columns, bay windows, and a wide bronze door all supported her comment. "And it's right on Lake Michigan," Bess added.

Beside us, the lake shimmered under sunny warm skies. Thanks to a light breeze, tiny whitecaps swirled over it as colorful sailboats skimmed the blue surface. After parking my car at a meter close to Jean-Georges's building, I said, "Alicia told me that Jean-Georges and Campbell own a triplex overlooking the lake. It combines work and living areas. The first floor is a showroom with Jean-Georges's work space behind it. They live on the second and third floors."

"I just hope the showroom is open," Bess said as we got out of the car.

Luckily, it was, and as Bess and I browsed through racks of clothes, I kept my eyes peeled for a man who might be Jean-Georges. But there was no man that I could see in the showroom at all, just one or two female shoppers and a salesgirl. I sighed, feeling frustrated. We'd come all this way to investigate Jean-Georges. What if he wasn't around?

I turned my attention to the clothes. They were beautifully made, with expensive fabrics and cuts, but they were different from what I'd expected—more streamlined than his lively, colorful designs that had appeared in that ten-year-old *Flair*. The main colors in the showroom were gray, brown, black, and white, and the outfits included more pants, jackets, and blouses than dresses. Everything here was much more subdued and tailored than Alicia's wild creations.

I scanned the room. There was a counter in the back with a cash register, and behind it was a door marked PRIVATE.

"I wonder what that door leads to," Bess asked, following my gaze.

"Probably to Jean-Georges's work space and their digs upstairs," I replied.

Suddenly the door swung open and a sportily

dressed couple strutted out. The man's thick blond-brown hair was held back in a ponytail; his white suit and suede bucks shone in the light from a nearby window. The woman's striking long platinum blond hair cascaded over her tall thin figure, and her gray miniskirt and white sleeveless blouse made her tanned skin glow. Gold bangles snaked around her left arm above the elbow. Since she looked exactly like the model, Campbell, in Ned's ten-year-old *Flair*, I figured white-suit guy was the hubby, Jean-Georges.

"He's a good six inches shorter than the blond chick," Bess observed. As she spoke, Jean-Georges zoomed up to the salesgirl behind the counter.

"Idiot!" he screamed. The girl, her face pale and frozen with terror, looked up at him in shock. "The Belmont Hotel told me they called and left a message with instructions for where to leave the clothes for the fashion show." Leaning toward her, he hissed, "So why didn't you give me that message?"

"I . . . I, well, the caller told me not to bother," she stammered. "He said he'd call back."

"Please, do not make that assumption again!" He strutted back to his wife. "Who hired her?" he asked, shrugging toward the salesgirl.

"I'll fire her for you right now, if you'd like," Campbell said. "Say the word, darling."

Jean-Georges smiled coldly at the salesgirl, who was quaking in terror. "Campbell, *cherie*, let's give the girl another chance. What do you say, Annie, or is it Amy? Do you deserve another chance?"

The girl said, "Allie. I'm sorry I didn't give you the message, Mr. de Vouvray. I'd thought he'd said . . ."

"Enough! We've heard your story already, Amy. Do better next time. Or else." Jean-Georges flicked his hand toward her in a dismissive gesture.

"This guy is ridiculous," Bess murmured. "I'd quit this second if I were that girl."

"She probably needs the money," I said sympathetically. "Jean-Georges is going to make such a pleasant dinner companion."

"Right!" Bess joked.

I squared my shoulders. "Well, if I can handle Mr. Tsao in a stuck elevator, I can handle Jean-Georges at a fancy dinner."

As we spoke, Campbell and Jean-Georges headed for the outside door.

"Bess," I whispered. "Do you mind if we leave the showroom for a little while? I can't decide whether to follow Campbell and Jean-Georges, or whether we should try to sneak into that private room, now that they're gone. Either choice means leaving here, though."

"No problem," Bess said agreeably. "But doesn't it make sense to follow them? We can always come back here and try to sneak through that door another time."

"Right on, Bess," I said. We made a beeline for the giant brass doors and slipped through them just before they swung closed behind Campbell and Jean-Georges. Once outside, the de Vouvrays clasped hands as Campbell towered above her husband, her sparkly flip-flops thwacking noisily as the two crossed the street against the light.

Bess and I hurried to catch up, but the traffic started moving just as we reached the corner. "I hope we don't lose them." I fixed my gaze on the pair as they headed down the opposite sidewalk and turned into an opening onto the beach.

After what seemed like forever, the traffic stopped. Bess and I jogged across the street, then picked up our pace as we approached the beach. Even though we could no longer see the de Vouvrays, we knew which direction they'd gone. I crossed my fingers they'd still be visible.

And they were! Once we'd turned onto the beach, the two were a hundred yards ahead of us, at a sailboat rental place. The red and white banner floating above the kiosk advertised its wares. Campbell and Jean-Georges weren't going anywhere—at least temporarily—and Bess and I were catching up to them, fast.

The hot sun beat down on us as the cloudless sky shimmered with heat, morphing into a dark violet blue at the horizon. If I hadn't been wearing sneakers, the sand would have scorched my feet. Bess, who had taken off her flip-flops to move faster over the sand, quickly put them back on.

"You'd think those two were newlyweds, the way they're carrying on," Bess said in disgust. It was true. Campbell and Jean-Georges couldn't keep their hands off each other, smooching and snuggling and hugging in an obnoxiously public way as they stood before the kiosk. "Ick," Bess added. "Don't get me wrong. I'm all for affection, but this is a bit extreme. Does the whole world need to see this?"

"Probably not," I agreed, wincing as the two clung to each other like vines.

A moment later, Bess and I had caught up, but the loving couple were too caught up in each other to notice us. Meanwhile, a small leathery man with deep wrinkles and a powder blue golf shirt called them over to the lake shore. After handing them life jackets, he helped them climb into a small sailboat moored nearby.

"Should we just wait here for them?" Bess asked.

"I wish I'd brought sunscreen. I don't want to clash with the red dress I'm wearing tonight. Alicia picked it out because it goes well with my skin tone."

I fished in my backpack and tossed Bess a tube of sunscreen. As she slathered it on, I said, "Bess, it's a beautiful day. Why wait here on shore? I've got some money to rent a boat—let's go." I asked the man renting sailboats whether he often rented to the de Vouvrays.

"They own their own boat," he explained. "I keep and maintain a few boats for special customers, but most of my business is rental." Glancing at the horizon, he added, "Now girls, don't lose sight of the beach. Afternoon thunderstorms are predicted, and the weather changes quickly on the lake."

I thanked him for his warning, and five minutes later, we were sailing across the blue water of Lake Michigan, being careful to keep the happy couple in our sights. But a light breeze and dazzling sunlight soon gave way to darkening skies and a whipping wind. "How did we get in the middle of a storm so quickly?" asked Bess anxiously as we tacked the sail to avoid being blown farther away from shore. "I mean, where has this storm been brewing? And where are Campbell and Jean-Georges?"

I scanned the water for them, but they seemed to

have vanished into the angry purple air surrounding us.

"And where's the coastline?" Bess asked. "Can you see it anymore, Nancy?"

I was too busy trying to control the sail to answer her, tightening the rope as the gale blew around us. Small swells had turned into large rollers, smacking upward against the sky. I bit my lip, praying I could keep the boat from tipping over.

11

Fashion Plate

The wind howled around us, and thunder and light-ning split the sky a few miles away. "We've got to keep this boat upright!" I yelled to Bess.

"Lower the sail, Nancy, don't tighten it," Bess cried, with her usual mechanics know-how—although her knowledge of boats came as a bit of a surprise. She grabbed the rope with me, and together we worked to lower the sail in the middle of the screeching wind. Waves tossed the tiny boat as if it was a piece of straw while we fought to keep our balance. With our muscles straining, we wrapped the rope around the dropped sail for safekeeping, and secured the boom so it wouldn't knock us off the boat. "We've done everything we can," Bess added, tightening her life jacket. "Let's just hope the center of the storm doesn't reach us."

But the black sky with its jagged explosions of lightning had moved even closer. There was no way the center of the storm would pass us by. And it would come in a matter of minutes, like a freight train bearing down on us. I didn't want to worry Bess by mentioning that once it arrived, lightning would strike the tallest point on the lake: us!

"Even if we could control this boat, we'd have no clue which direction to take," Bess declared. "The coastline is anyone's guess."

A faint noise like a sick seagull came through the storm. It grew stronger. Someone was screaming for help. "Do you hear that, Bess?"

"Look!" Bess cried, as a hazy red form took shape ahead of us. "It's an overturned sailboat with someone clinging to it."

As we got closer to the boat, I saw that it was *two* someones—Campbell and Jean-Georges—hanging desperately onto the hull. Campbell's feet, minus her flip-flops, kicked and thrashed, while her husband's legs had sunk into the water, as if he had given up hope. They obviously needed to be rescued fast, but how could we do that without dooming ourselves? The slightest extra weight on the gunwales would tip us over in one second flat.

Still, we had to try.

"Hey!" I called. "When our boat blows against

yours, let's try to get you on board. Good thing you've got on your life vests."

At the sound of my voice, Jean-Georges came alive with a jolt, whipping his head toward us. Campbell did the opposite. She stopped kicking and sagged against their boat. "Thank goodness!" she cried.

I gritted my teeth, trying not to imagine the four of us stranded in the water, beyond help, our two boats overturned. But just as our boat was close enough for Bess and me to reach out to the shipwrecked pair, the roar of a motorboat cut through the storm.

I froze, then shouted for help—even though no one could hear me over the engine's whine. A Coast Guard motorboat zoomed into view. I'd never appreciated that sound so much!

Minutes later, the four of us sat huddled in blankets inside the motorboat as our two Coast Guard rescuers sped toward shore. Campbell, with her long blond hair wet and snarled, and her miniskirt shrunken even minier, looked totally freaked. She basically clammed up while Jean-Georges held forth on a number of subjects. "It was folly, *folly* I tell you, not to check the weather before venturing out on the lake," he declared in a heavy French accent to no one in particular.

"Lake Michigan is known for storms coming out of nowhere," I said. "That's what the boat rental guy told us."

"You're right, my dear. I've lived for years with a stunning view of the magnificent ocean they call Lake Michigan," he said grandly. "From my beautiful loft, I've studied the lake in its many moods. I know how unpredictable the weather out there can be."

"We should never have come out," Campbell moaned.

"Not true, my dear, not true," Jean-Georges retorted. "For if we hadn't come out, we would never have met these two lovely and courageous young ladies. I pledge eternal gratitude to you Nancy, and you Bess, for saving our hides. By the way, are you ladies from Chicago?"

"River Heights," Bess said, before I could stop her.

But Jean-Georges didn't bat an eye. "Just so you know how sincere my feelings are," he went on, "I hope you girls will accept my invitation to join us back at our loft for a hot shower and a cup of mocha latte—a specialty of mine. You don't want to wander the city in wet clothes."

"We'd love to!" Bess declared. I tossed her a smile. This invitation was worth every scary, wet moment leading up to it. What better way to scope out Jean-Georges than to be invited into his private home?

Once on the third floor of the de Vouvrays' loft, Bess used the guest room shower while I used the one off the master bedroom. Jean-Georges had even given us a couple of his outfits for free so we wouldn't have to wear our wet clothes. Mine was a bleached denim skirt, a peach-colored scoop-necked T-shirt with a picture of a giant peach on the front, and sandals with straps studded with fake turquoise. Bess's was similar, except her T-shirt was black with a picture of a white cat curled on the front. "My most youthful separates!" Jean-Georges had crowed as he handed them to us. "Not like my boring corporate clothes that make women look like men," he'd added, scowling in the general direction of his showroom.

Upstairs, I showered in two seconds flat, determined to put the rest of my time to good use. I wanted to snoop before the de Vouvrays missed me, so after dressing I got to work poking around the master bedroom.

First stop, Jean-Georges's bureau. In my experience, bureaus are gold mines of clues and valuable info—and Jean-Georges's bureau did not disappoint. Hidden under some scarves in the top drawer was a box filled with letters, but the one that caught my eye said "Alicia Adams" on the return address. I opened it up.

Interesting. Alicia had written to Jean-Georges that all Swoon designs were hers alone, she had never copied anything of his, and most important, she'd saved all her original work on her laptop with authentic dates on the files, so she could prove that her designs

110

predated his. In fact, Jean-Georges was the one who had ripped her off! How dare he accuse her of stealing from him?

So Alicia *had* set him straight.

Steps approached in the hallway outside the closed door to the master bedroom. I shoved the letter back into its envelope and replaced it neatly in the box.

Jean-Georges poked his head through the door just as I yanked my hand out of his drawer. Ouch!

"Nancy!" he said. "So sorry to intrude."

"Jean-Georges, *I'm* so sorry." I gently slid the drawer shut. "I was, uh, looking for a hairbrush. Would Campbell mind if I used hers?"

"Probably, but we'll keep it our secret," he said with a wink. His mood change was remarkable; he didn't seem at all like the man we'd first seen shouting in the showroom. "Her dresser is over there," he said pointing to the facing wall, where a pink frilly dresser was littered with make-up.

"Oh, of course, my mistake. Sorry."

"That's quite all right. Again, accept my apologies for intruding. I thought you'd already joined the others."

"I'm keeping you from your shower," I said, feeling a stab of guilt at the sight of his damp suit and wet hair. His bare feet looked blue with cold as I bustled by him, carrying my wet clothes. "I think I might have a comb in my backpack somewhere."

"Thank you, Nancy. As soon as I'm warm and dry, I'll have everyone set up with a mocha latte."

Soon we were all settled in the de Vouvrays' fabulous living room overlooking the lake, sipping mocha lattes as the sun broke through the storm clouds. The water below us glittered as if a zillion jewels had been flung onto it, sending prisms of light careening through the giant plate glass windows of the loft. There was no doubt in my mind that Jean-Georges had a pretty great life. Like Alicia, he was super successful. So why would he bother to take revenge on her?

Bess and I explained to the de Vouvrays that we would be at the Awards Dinner tonight, too, but I knew better than to mention Alicia. Jean-Georges would boot us out of here pronto if he knew we were friends with her, and I must say I was enjoying my mocha latte, the view, and the chance to observe Jean-Georges up close in his home with his defenses down.

But no juicy tidbits of info came my way other than Alicia's letter, and soon Bess and I thanked the de Vouvrays and said good-bye. On our way to the Belmont Hotel, though, I wanted to talk to Bess about his odd mood change. "Even though Jean-Georges was nice to us," I said, turning to Bess, "we've seen how he's capable of behaving. Remember the way he treated his assistant?"

Beside me in the car, Bess nodded. "I'm sure he wouldn't hesitate to treat Alicia badly, either," she commented.

At the hotel, Bess headed for the runway rehearsal while I went straight to our room to unpack. Just as I was slipping my card key into the lock, Alicia stepped out of the room next door. "Nancy!" she said, smiling. "Great to see you. I'm off to the rehearsal, but I'll catch you later."

"Hang on, I want to fill you in on some interesting findings," I said, quickly telling her about my trip to the de Vouyrays' pad. I also told her about finding her letter to Jean-Georges.

"Yes," she went on. "I wrote him that letter to set the record straight and get him off my back. I'm grateful I still have my laptop with the dates on my old files to prove my designs predate Jean-Georges's. In case he ever decides to sue. Thank goodness the vandals didn't take it from Swoon 2."

"So you keep your laptop at Swoon 2?" I asked.

"I used to keep it at the Chicago Swoon, but since I've been spending more time at the new store lately, I brought it with me for safekeeping."

"Hmm," I said, stopping myself from going further. I made a mental note to ask Alicia to check that those files were still on her laptop—could they really be safe?—but I didn't want to worry her before the banquet.

Once at the banquet, I found myself seated next to Jean-Georges, who was chatting up a famous model sitting on his other side. Too bad. No chance to question him. At least the dinner was delicious—duck with cherry sauce. The fashion show that followed was even better, with the clothes getting more flamboyant and wild as each model swished by. Bess glowed on the runway in Alicia's awesome designs. Even Charlie Adams had come to root for his older sister. The whole event was glamorous, filled with beautiful people wearing beautiful clothes. Alicia had lent me a strapless dress of mango-colored silk, with a scattering of violet-tinted glass beads sewn across the front, to go with my strawberry blond hair.

The crew from *Threads* fluttered around the enormous room, except for Ned and a few other interns who were staffing the home office. I caught a glimpse of Natalie, hands on hips, scolding Deirdre while Deirdre faced her with a knowing smirk. Most interns would show more humility to their bosses, but not Deirdre. And, by the way, how did Deirdre luck out and get to be here instead of holding down the fort with the other interns in River Heights?

I didn't want to know!

After the fashion show, the judges announced the winners from a dais up front. A reed-thin older woman sheathed in a gold dress, her ink-black hair in a bun, spoke into the microphone. "And the winner of the bronze medal is Delia Santiago," she intoned. Applause filled the enormous room as a young woman cheerfully accepted her award. Once she'd stepped down, the older woman continued, "And the silver medal goes to . . . Jean-Georges de Vouvray."

Jean-Georges shot up from his seat on my right, looking both pleased and annoyed. He seemed happy to have won something, but miffed that he hadn't won gold. By the time he'd strutted to the podium, he'd plastered on a fake smile and graciously accepted his award.

Once he was seated again, the announcer adjusted her microphone, and a hush fell over the room. "Last but not least," she sang out as the audience chuckled nervously, "the gold medal. Alicia Adams, would you please come up here to accept your award?"

Applause drowned out all speech as Alicia swept her way up to the podium. Next to me, Jean-Georges's brows knitted together, and a seething sound came from between his clenched teeth. I wasn't worried he'd explode like Mr. Tsao had in the elevator yesterday—I knew Jean-Georges had more self-control than that—but I also could tell that he was feeling every bit as angry.

"Hello darling," a voice said on my left. Turning, I met Deirdre's jubilant gaze. "Nancy, if you're here to solve the mystery of the stuff that went down at Swoon 2," she said, "you might as well give up now. I'm this close to breaking the case." She held her thumb and forefinger a quarter inch apart.

"Deirdre, I'm here to support Alicia," I said, "and Bess, too."

Deirdre sniffed. "Bess could use support. She was a disaster on the runway, if you ask me. Alicia's clothes aren't made for teenage girls. They're for older, more sophisticated women." She sighed, adding, "Just wait, Nancy. After I break this case, Chief McGinnis will look to *me* to solve crimes in River Heights. He'll be *so* disappointed in you."

"I don't work for Chief McGinnis, Deirdre. I solve mysteries for myself," I said.

"Maybe so," Deirdre said smugly, "but I know you want to beat me on this one."

As Deirdre pranced away, dessert was served. Saved by the chocolate and vanilla layered mousse! I glanced in relief at my square of mousse cake—then did a major double take. A tiny blue-iced butterfly gleamed up at me from the glaze of chocolate covering the top.

12

One Sweet Clue

Okay. I glanced at Jean-Georges's mousse on my right. Other than a tiny mint leaf, no decoration there. Ditto for the one on my left, and for every other one at my table.

As my eyes took in the other mousses, Jean-Georges began devouring his. He didn't even try to sneak a glance my way. Shouldn't he be more interested in my reaction to the butterfly? Unless he wasn't guilty.

Still, he was sitting right next to me, with plenty of opportunity for mischief. Could he have sneaked the mousse onto the table while I wasn't looking?

I glanced at the servers darting around the zillions of circular tables in the banquet hall. After spooning off the top of my mousse so as not to draw attention to the butterfly, I excused myself from the table and went in search of our server. I cornered him on his way to the kitchen, several feet from the swinging door. "Uh, would you mind answering a quick question?" I asked politely.

"Certainly," he said, just as politely.

"You served me a piece of chocolate mousse with a blue butterfly on the top. But no one else got one like it. Did someone ask you to serve it to me?"

"Yes, miss," he replied. "Someone wrote an anonymous note asking that this particular mousse go to the young lady with strawberry blond hair sitting next to Jean-Georges de Vouvray."

"An anonymous note, huh?"

"Yes, miss." An anxious expression suddenly crossed his face. "Is everything all right, miss? I just assumed it was your birthday or something, and that the butterfly was special to you and your admirer. I hope I didn't act out of line." He fished in his pocket and drew out a note. "Please, take a look."

The message was written in a flowery script with large round letters—a woman's, I guessed. Or a man's if he wanted to hide his identity. My eyes met the server's. "Can I keep this?"

"Sure. As I said, I hope I did the right thing."

Sticking the note in my purse, I smiled at him. "You did fine. Thanks so much."

As I returned to my table, Natalie Stephanoff

sashayed by me in a low-cut turquoise gown, butterfly aquamarines glittering on her earlobes. My gaze fixed on her.

No question Natalie was a schmoozer. She flitted around the tables like a real butterfly, greeting this person and that person, air-kissing everyone in sight. Hmm. Just a hunch, but maybe I was missing an opportunity here. I mean, shouldn't I be searching Natalie's office in River Heights while she and Deirdre were partying in Chicago? Taking my cell phone from my purse, I headed into a quiet corridor off the banquet hall and speed-dialed Ned.

"Nancy!" he said on the first ring. "Any news?"

"Hi, Ned, could you get me into the *Threads* offices first thing tomorrow morning before the other interns come in? Say, seven a.m.? I know it's a lot to ask. It's so early, I mean."

"Anything to help you solve this mystery, Nancy," Ned said gamely. "Thank you so much. I miss you tonight. See you at *Threads* tomorrow."

I flipped my phone shut, feeling incredibly lucky to have a boyfriend who doesn't mind dragging himself out of bed two hours early to help me with a case.

Back at the party, people had started to mingle again, having finished dessert. Alicia was at the center of well-wishers; even so, she found time to say hi to me. At her side was an attractive young woman wearing a lemon-colored dress that complemented her dark skin.

I wanted to ask Alicia whether she'd noticed Natalie's earrings, but Alicia spoke first. "Nancy," she said, "I want you to meet Rosina Lewis, my publicity agent." Immediately after Rosina and I shook hands, Alicia was carried away by a tide of friends and colleagues, leaving us two to talk.

"Rosina, I've been wanting to meet you," I said. "Alicia mentioned that you never publicized the sale at Swoon 2."

"That's true," Rosina said firmly. "I have no idea how those announcements got into *Threads* or the *River Heights Bugle*, or on the radio, either. See, both Alicia and I thought word-of-mouth publicity would be plenty. Neither of us wanted the kind of crazy scene that happened last Friday at the store."

"Do you have any idea who could have sent in those notices?"

Rosina shook her head. "No idea at all. I hope Alicia believes me, Nancy, but I'm just as confused as she is about this. I don't get who would go to the trouble of publicizing a sale when it wasn't even their store."

"Someone who wanted to make trouble for Alicia," I replied. "I just wish I knew who that person was."

After saying good-bye to Rosina, I made my way to Natalie, who was blithely air-kissing a cluster of young people. I tapped Natalie's shoulder as the group melted into the crowd. "Yes?" she said coldly. "Have we met?"

"Not officially. I'm Nancy Drew, Ned Nickerson's girlfriend. You know, he's interning in the photo department at *Threads*?"

"Yes, of course. I know Ned. He does very nice work. Anyway, what can I do for you, Nancy?" Natalie was not unpleasant, just brisk and businesslike. So I got down to business, too.

"*Threads* printed a notice of the sale at Swoon 2 a few days before it happened," I explained. "The *River Heights Bugle* did the same thing, and some local radio stations also announced it. But Alicia Adams never sent out press releases or bought ads. Do you know who printed the notice in *Threads*?"

Natalie's chin shot up defiantly. "I put the notice in *Threads*, though of course I had nothing to do with the *Bugle* or the radio announcements. Why do you care, anyway?"

I shrugged. "I'm just helping Alicia figure out why things went so wrong at her sale. The main reason seems to be unwanted publicity."

"Well, *I* thought I'd be doing her a favor by publicizing it. I first heard about the sale from Charlie Adams, Alicia's own brother. If she didn't want anyone to know about it, then she shouldn't have told anyone. Some sale that would have been," Natalie added, rolling her eyes.

"Yes, but too much publicity didn't work, either," I reminded her. "Anyway, thanks for the info. Nice earrings, Natalie. Does Alicia know you've borrowed them?"

"Of course she does," Natalie said, shooting me a scowl as she walked away.

The party was winding down as I told Bess my decision to leave at the crack of dawn tomorrow to meet Ned at *Threads*. Bess said, "I'll just catch a ride home with Alicia. She's planning to check on her Chicago store tomorrow morning before leaving, so I'll have a chance to sleep in while she's doing that."

"After helping both me and Alicia today, Bess, you deserve a rest," I said. "Speaking of which, I'm heading upstairs now for some snoozing myself. I want to be as alert as possible tomorrow. I'll see you back in River Heights."

Bess and I hugged good night, and before long I was falling asleep in my comfy hotel bed, excited about tomorrow.

Promptly at seven, Ned let me into the *Threads* offices with his passkey. "Thanks, Ned," I said. "Maybe you should leave now so you won't get blamed if I'm caught snooping."

Ned frowned. I could tell he didn't like the idea of me alone here in these empty offices, which were spooky this early in the morning with no one else around. "Nancy, I'd rather get busted for letting you in than have something happen to you here without me."

I smiled at him. "Ned, this is a fashion magazine. What could possibly happen to me? Plus Natalie is the main suspect here, and she's a couple hours away in Chicago, sleeping off her late night partying. I'll be fine, I promise."

Ned shot me a doubtful look. "Okay, Nancy. If you're sure."

"I'm sure. I don't want you to lose your job." I turned to head down a hall, then stopped short. "Oh, Ned, one more thing. Do you know what Natalie's computer password is?"

"She likes to call herself 'fashion chick' around the office. That's how she thinks of herself, and it's sort of become her nickname. It's just an educated guess, but you might try it."

"Okay, thanks Ned. See you soon," I said.

Soon I was alone, logging on to Natalie's files thanks to Ned's educated guess. "Fashion chick" it was, and after a few moments of checking Natalie's e-mail in-box, I began to scroll through her sent messages.

I blinked in surprise. Not only was there an e-mail

to the *River Heights Bugle*, but there was another one to the local radio station. Both messages announced Swoon 2's sale.

I sat back in Natalie's swivel chair, staring at the messages. Why did Natalie lie to me? And what was the deal with the butterfly earrings? And what else did Deirdre have on Natalie?

A floorboard creaked outside the office door. I jolted upright—to see none other than Dierdre, notepad in hand.

13

Dangerous Designs

Ned is so busted!" Deirdre exclaimed. "I can't wait to tell his boss he let you in. Ned'll lose his job, for sure."

"There's no way you can prove Ned let me in," I said. "Plus, if you threaten to tell on Ned, I can always say I caught you checking out earrings in Natalie's desk drawer."

Deirdre blanched. "Natalie is history here, anyway. She won't have power over me for very much longer. She's obviously Alicia's vandal. I just need one more piece of evidence tying her to the scene of the crime before I go to Chief McGinnis and turn her in." Her green eyes snapped with glee. "Won't she be surprised?"

Note to self: Never hire Deirdre Shannon as an assistant. "I guess loyalty isn't your thing, Deirdre," I commented.

"Why should I be loyal to Natalie, when she was so bossy to me? Serves her right. She shouldn't vandalize places and still be allowed this cushy job."

I studied Deirdre curiously. "What evidence do you have on Natalie anyway, Deirdre? I mean, what do you think her motive is for hurting Alicia?"

Deirdre smirked. "I've told you zillions of times, Nancy, I'm not revealing what I've found. Especially to you. You're my competition, in case you've forgotten."

"Fine." I turned my attention back to the computer screen and scrolled through more sent e-mails to double check that I hadn't missed anything. An e-mail from Natalie to Alicia dated last Thursday, the day before Swoon 2 opened, popped out at me. Curious, I clicked on it.

In a friendly, bubbly style, Natalie asked Alicia whether she could borrow the butterfly earrings until after the Fashion Awards Dinner. "They'd be a fab match with the dress I'm planning to wear," Natalie wrote. "Be a darling to this poor magazine reporter who worships your designs, and I'll be in your debt forever. Any favorable press I can give you, Alicia my dear, is yours for the asking."

I clicked on Natalie's in-box to double check the

messages she'd received in recent days. Was there anything from Alicia responding to Natalie's request? My eyes scanned the monitor.

Nope. Nothing.

Maybe Alicia had been so busy with the events at Swoon 2 that she'd never read Natalie's e-mail. One thing was for sure, Natalie obviously hadn't meant to steal the earrings she was wearing.

Deirdre was still loitering in the doorway, probably waiting for me to leave so she could do some snooping herself. I called her over to Natalie's computer. "Look at this e-mail," I told her. "Natalie wrote to Alicia asking if she could borrow the butterfly earrings. So the earrings you found in Natalie's desk were probably not the ones lifted from Swoon 2. Which makes it less likely that she was the vandal."

Deirdre's face turned pale, but she said nothing. I decided to press her. "Deirdre, I don't believe you have any other evidence against Natalie. That's why you refused to tell me what you know. You know no more than I do!"

"Not . . . true!" Deirdre sputtered, her eyes flashing. "I've got tons of evidence, tons."

"My bet is you're here for the same reason I am," I said. "You thought it would be a safe time to investigate Natalie while she's in Chicago. You're hoping to find some evidence against her."

"No, no, I'm here to . . . do work," Deirdre said lamely. "Natalie asked me to the Awards Dinner last night because her regular assistant got sick. I'm here to type my notes for her."

"You drove down from Chicago at this crazy hour just to type notes?" I asked.

Uncertainty flickered in Deirdre's eyes. "Okay, okay, have it your way, Nancy," she snapped. "It's true—I have nothing on Natalie to connect her with the vandalism except for the butterfly earrings I found in her desk."

"Which we know Natalie didn't steal," I said.

"Yes, yes," Deirdre said, sounding exasperated. "You don't have to rub it in."

"So why were you searching her desk in the first place if you had no evidence against her? What made you suspicious?" I asked.

"Nothing. I was looking for a pen."

"Deirdre, we both know that's not true. Remember, I found you holding the earrings. Why should I keep your secret if you're not going to tell me the truth?"

"You really are persistent, Nancy," Deirdre said, rolling her eyes. "If you absolutely must know, I overheard Natalie asking certain news outlets to keep mum that she'd told them about the Swoon 2 opening. I thought that was sort of strange, so I decided to do some investigating. First, I was curious to know why Natalie leaked the news of the sale, and second, why she wanted her leak to be so hush hush. It was while I was investigating her—I refuse to call it snooping," she added haughtily, "that I discovered the earrings."

"I agree it's strange that Natalie leaked Alicia's sale to other news places, but most interns wouldn't connect that to the vandalism and start investigating their boss," I observed. "I mean, don't you like working for Natalie?"

"Actually, I can't stand her!" Deirdre blurted. "She's so bossy. I started snooping—okay, *snooping*—because I wanted something to hold over her. I think she's getting ready to fire me!"

"Really? Why?"

Deirdre's faced flushed, whether with anger or shame I wasn't sure. "She claims I'm not willing to do things her way. That I think my own ideas are better. Which they are!"

I sighed. I was tempted to remind Deirdre that Natalie was still her boss. But why waste my words? They wouldn't sink in. Instead, I said, "Now that we know Natalie didn't steal the earrings, there's really not much evidence against her."

"Yeah, but why did she tell those news outlets about the sale?" Deirdre asked.

"None of your business!" snapped a voice behind us.

I swung Natalie's swivel chair around to meet her furious eyes.

"Natalie!" Deirdre croaked.

"Deirdre, did you let Nancy in?" Natalie asked.

"Ned Nickerson did," Deirdre said, "her boyfriend."

"Then I'll fire him today," Natalie said.

"Ned's boss is the photo editor, not you, Natalie," I said. "Something tells me you don't have that authority."

Natalie spun toward Deirdre. "Ungrateful girl! I heard everything you said about me. Get!" Even though Natalie was shorter, she seemed to tower over Deirdre as she pointed a commanding finger toward the office door. As Deirdre slunk out, Natalie added, "You're a disgrace to both journalism and fashion. Never darken the doorway of this magazine again."

Quickly, I logged out of Natalie's files. I'd decided I'd better level with her. I mean, I was in *her* chair.

I stood, then moved toward the door, keeping a respectful distance from her. "Look, Natalie, I'm really sorry," I said. "You have every right to toss me out of here, too. But I was hoping for your help investigating the vandalism at Swoon 2. I think we'd both like to help Alicia. She's so talented, and she's going to go really far. Plus, she's become a friend of mine."

Natalie narrowed her eyes. I could tell she was torn. On the one hand, she'd caught me sitting in her desk chair staring at her computer screen. On the other hand, Alicia was totally cool and famous, and I was her friend.

Indecision flickered across Natalie's face, and I held my breath. She lowered her eyes. And then she raised them to mine and smiled. "How can I help Alicia?" she asked.

"By telling me the truth. Why did you give other news outlets info about the Swoon 2 sale?"

"That was such a mistake," Natalie said, shaking her head. "If only I could go back in time and stop myself from interfering. See, I wanted to make sure there would be a big story for me to write about when I covered the opening and sale. I thought if the story were really major, my article would get more attention. Alicia wasn't publicizing her sale, which I thought was a mistake because if no one came to it, no one would care about the coverage. I had no idea the publicity would make the sale such a mob scene. But I guessed wrong. Alicia was right. She knows her store and her market, and I goofed. That's the simple truth. I feel really bad."

"Well, don't beat yourself up about it too much, Natalie," I said. "You didn't know. But as you say, Alicia does know her stuff. It's her business."

"Sometimes I can be too much of a workaholic," Natalie declared. "That's why I came down from

Chicago so early—to start my story about the Awards Dinner. Anyway, I owe Alicia a good deed. Make that *many* good deeds. You can be my witness, Nancy, that from now on, I'm writing nothing but positive things about Alicia's designs for the rest of her career. May it be a long one."

"Just write the truth," I suggested. "I think she'll be happy with that. Anyway, we have to find out who's been hurting her store so she can get on with her life." I paused. "Did you know that a pair of earrings just like the ones you wore last night were taken from Swoon 2?"

Natalie looked shocked. "No kidding! Alicia reminded me, in a nice way, that the earrings I wore last night belonged to Swoon 2. I'd e-mailed her to ask permission to wear them, but I guess she missed my message." Natalie shrugged. "I gave them back to her at the end of the party last night."

"I'm sure she's happy to have at least one pair back," I said dryly. While we stood by Natalie's office door, people began to trickle into work, strolling down the corridor holding paper coffee cups and calling out hellos.

Time to leave. For one thing, I didn't want Ned to find me talking to Natalie. Awkward! He'd assume she'd caught me—which of course was the truth. He also might think he was in trouble. An embarrassed or guilty Ned would make me sad, especially when he'd been such a big help.

I thanked Natalie for her honesty and returned to my car, which I'd parked on River Street at a meter I'd forgotten to plug. Phew—no ticket. I tend to forget about things like that when I'm on a case. Speaking of which: some case! I was back to square one. All my suspects seemed to be red herrings except for Jean-Georges.

Then, like lightning, a sudden horrible thought flashed through my head. I had to talk to Alicia ASAP!

I called her cell phone from my parked car. No answer. Once home, I ate breakfast, and then called Swoon 2 as soon as it opened and left a message with her sales assistant for Alicia to call me. By mid-afternoon, Alicia returned my call, having just arrived at Swoon 2 from Chicago.

"Do you have a minute, Alicia?" I asked. "I'd like to come over to the store."

"Of course, Nancy," she answered. "Any time."

When I arrived, I found Alicia arranging racks of clothes. Fortunately, there weren't too many customers. "Alicia," I began, keeping my voice low, "your old laptop—the one with the designs Jean-Georges claims are his—that's still here, right?" When she nodded, I went on, "Have you made sure the old design files are still on it?"

Her horrified look told me the answer. She scooted over to the register and bent down. With shaky fingers, she lifted the laptop out of a drawer beneath the counter and booted it up. After a moment of scrolling and clicking, Alicia turned stricken eyes to mine. "The files aren't here," she whispered.

Grimly, she fumbled again in the drawer, then yanked it so hard that it flew out of its groove, its contents spilling onto the floor. Alicia studied the pens, Post-its, and other supplies, her face pale as a ghost's. "I keep backup disks in a pouch. They're gone, too! I hadn't thought to look for them till now. I mean, with all the stuff going on here, the disks hadn't been on my mind."

"Don't blame yourself, Alicia. Blame Jean-Georges."

"What do we do next?" she asked.

"Return to Chicago. Can your sales assistant cover for you here?"

Soon Alicia had arranged for her assistant to manage Swoon 2 for the rest of the afternoon, and we were zooming down the freeway back toward Chicago. As I drove, I filled Alicia in about details of the case that she might not know, like the butterfly surprise on my chocolate mousse and what I'd learned from Natalie.

Once at Jean-Georges's showroom, we learned

from the salesgirl that the de Vouvrays were attending a small post–Fashion Awards cocktail party.

"Jean-Georges is such a big socialite," Alicia murmured, out of the salesgirl's hearing. "I'm not surprised he's partying this evening. I was invited to that party, too, along with Delia the bronze medal winner, but after the Awards Dinner last night, I've had enough celebrating to last me for the month!"

"Jean-Georges seems to love it," I commented.

Alicia shrugged. "Don't get me wrong—I enjoy talking to people and having a good time, but this constant socializing can be a bit much. That's the life of a fashion designer, but I need time to make clothes."

"Oh, *that*," I said, teasing. "But seriously, Alicia, let's see if we can find those disks. The salesgirl is over there now with other customers." I nodded toward the far side of the large room. Racks of clothes gave us some protection from her view.

Alicia and I quickly searched the drawers behind the counter. No pouch, no disks. "See that door?" I asked, pointing at the PRIVATE sign. "Hope it's not locked."

We glanced toward the salesgirl to make sure she wasn't looking. Then we hurried through the unlocked door.

A quick scan of Jean-Georges's workroom was a bust, so we headed upstairs. Searching the de Vouvrays' house was the opposite of searching Bettina's, since the de Vouvrays' style was super spare. Cabinet drawers held perfectly placed kitchenware, study drawers contained neat boxes of office supplies, and the antique chest in the living room was empty of clutter. There just weren't many places to search.

"Let's check Jean-Georges's bedroom," I said, pointing up the staircase to the third floor. "I didn't get to finish yesterday."

Once upstairs, I paused, listening. Something was wrong. Some sound. I grabbed Alicia's arm to stop her as we rounded the door of the master bedroom.

A soft snoring noise floated up from the bed. We tiptoed closer. And then we saw Campbell sprawled over the sheets, her long blond hair across the pillow, butterfly earrings twinkling on her ears.

Alicia and I exchanged looks. "So did *she* steal the earrings from Swoon 2," I whispered, "or did Jean-Georges steal them to give to her? Could *she* be the vandal?"

Alicia shrugged. "Maybe she acted with Jean-Georges's blessing."

A fat white cat sleeping at the foot of the bed jolted awake, focusing suspicious blue eyes on us. It leaped up, opened its mouth, and let out a piercing wail that filled the room like a siren. Campbell shot awake.

She stared at us, bewildered, propped up on her hands. Her hair, knotted and mussed, cascaded over her shoulders, making her look like a combo of Sleeping Beauty and Rapunzel. And the wicked witch.

The dawning look of understanding in Campbell's eyes morphed into spite as she snapped up a bottle of nail polish remover by her bed. Shooting us a sly smile, she took off the top.

The fumes snaked around us. "Welcome, girls," she snarled. "I have a special beauty treatment for you." She drew back her hand, ready to hurl the blinding liquid at our faces.

14

Stylish Solutions

Alicia, duck!" I cried, hitting the floor. But Alicia stood frozen in shock as Campbell let the liquid fly. "Alicia! She'll blind you." I tackled her to the ground in the nick of time. Or almost in the nick of time, since a small patch of her auburn hair glistened with the poisonous liquid.

The fumes surrounded us. I focused on Campbell's ice-blue eyes, the same color as her cat's, and the butterfly earrings. "So you took the earrings, Campbell," I began. "You were in on all this—vandalizing Swoon 2 and deleting the files. You and Jean-Georges together. Or just you?"

Campbell threw me a scathing look before picking up the phone on her bedside table and punching

911. "I've got intruders in my house," she yelled into the receiver.

After giving the dispatcher her address, she slammed the phone down, picked it up again, and began dialing—Jean-Georges, I guessed. But I couldn't let her talk to him before I asked her some questions.

My mind clicked back to Alicia mentioning that she and Campbell had been roommates in Paris in their modeling days. Maybe there was some ancient love-triangle grudge Campbell held against Alicia. I mean, that wasn't such a crazy thought—Campbell *had* married Alicia's old boyfriend.

I lunged for the phone, but Campbell waved it wildly back and forth, trying her best to keep it from me. "How dare you?" she screeched. "You're attacking me in my own house. Help, someone, intruders!"

I grabbed the phone, but she wouldn't let it go without a battle. With a quick surprise twist, I wrestled it from her hands. "Campbell," I said, "okay, we're intruders here, but you trespassed at Swoon 2. And trashed it! Before we ever came here! The police will be much more impressed by your crime than by ours."

"My cell phone," she muttered, searching through rumpled bedcovers.

"Campbell, listen," I began, hoping I could somehow get her to answer one question. "Why did you and Jean-Georges go into Swoon 2, destroy the place, and steal earrings and computer files? We just want to know why."

Campbell looked at me, her eyes glazed with confusion and fear. Tears sprang into them and spilled over, streaking down her cheeks as she burst into choking sobs. Dropping her face into her hands, she wailed, "Jean-Georges is innocent. I am entirely to blame." Her gasps made the rest of her words impossible to understand.

I turned to Alicia, who was staring at Campbell in disbelief. "I've never seen this side of her," she murmured.

"Alicia," I said, "is there some piece of ancient history I'm not getting? I mean, about the three of you?"

Alicia looked baffled. "I'll tell you all I know, Nancy. I just hope I'll be able to shed some light, because I'm pretty confused myself."

"Okay, shoot," I said, hoping to encourage her.

As Campbell continued to weep uncontrollably, Alicia began her story. "Even though this happened ten years ago, just thinking about it again makes that time seem so recent," she mused. "Anyway, since

Campbell and I were both American models from the same state, we decided to room together in Paris. But those things weren't all we had in common. We had Jean-Georges. Once Jean-Georges's and my relationship cooled, Campbell swooped in to snag him for herself. But why Campbell would want to hurt my store a decade later, I can't even guess."

"I can guess," I said. "Campbell deleted your files and stole your disks to get rid of evidence. The evidence that your designs predate his."

The moment I spoke those words, Campbell's wails grew louder—racking, heaving sobs that drowned out our voices. I pulled Alicia back from the bed so that I could hear her better.

Alicia asked, "But what about the vandalism? Why did she scrawl those messages? And did she have to ruin my dress?"

"I bet the vandalism was just a distraction from the theft," I said. "Campbell didn't want us to realize those files and disks were missing, so she covered up that crime by trashing the store. And she made us all think it was PFAF that was guilty by writing all those messages. Maybe Campbell was mad at PFAF for some reason and saw a chance for payback."

"But what about the butterfly earrings?" Alicia asked.

I shrugged. "I bet she took the earrings as an after-thought just because she liked them. Campbell prob-ably realized I was helping you after Bess mentioned we were from River Heights and Jean-Georges found me snooping in his bureau; he must have told her about it. I bet Campbell was just trying to tease me by putting a butterfly on my chocolate mousse at the Awards Dinner. My investigation was probably like a cat and mouse game to her."

Alicia frowned. "All that makes sense, but here's what I don't get. Why did Campbell care about delet-ing my files when they affected Jean-Georges's work, not hers?" Alicia's eyes met mine as she added, "To help his case?"

Campbell shot up from the bed. With her long uncombed hair, tear-streaked face, and wild red eyes, she looked like a madwoman. "Jean-Georges had nothing to do with my crime," she shrieked. "How many times do I have to repeat myself?" She sighed heavily, then slumped back down on the bed. "Okay, if you promise not to tell Jean-Georges and not to press charges, I'll tell you anything you want. Anything."

"The truth will be fine," I said. Turning to Alicia, I added, "The decision is yours. But if we don't prom-ise, then Campbell won't spill her story, and we won't have any evidence tying her to the vandalism anyway. So we're in sort of a bind."

"I see your point, Nancy. I'm curious to know what she has to say." Alicia turned to Campbell. "I'll promise not to press charges against you, Campbell, if you return my disks and earrings—and make Jean-Georges stop saying I copied him."

"I'll try my hardest. I suppose I have some influence over him." Campbell shuffled over to her frilly pink dresser and, with a key, opened a drawer hidden underneath the ruffles. She removed a dark blue pouch, took off the earrings, and dropped them inside before handing it to Alicia. Then she went on. "Okay, if you want the truth, here it is. Ten years ago when we lived in Paris, I first caught Jean-Georges's attention by supplying him with some of your early designs, Alicia. Remember the designs you'd sketch on the side while you were still a model? You'd spend long hours copying them onto your computer. I told Jean-Georges they were mine."

Silence hung in the room for a moment as Alicia took in Campbell's words. "So you pretended my designs were yours," she said. "Which is why Jean-Georges thought the Swoon designs were copies of his, instead of the other way around."

"Yes," Campbell said sheepishly. "You told me you'd

never shown them to anyone else but me because you felt shy about them. So I knew Jean-Georges had never seen them. My plan worked—up to a point. Jean-Georges was so impressed by the designs that his interest in me kept building. It's not that he loved me for the designs, but they were a way to keep him calling me at first. Then, after he got to know me, he really did fall in love and we got married."

"So did you offer Jean-Georges the designs, or was it his idea to use them as his own?" Alicia asked.

"His idea," Campbell explained. "He wanted to use them for one of his first collections. I said yes, not thinking you would ever be successful on your own, or that you would realize you'd been ripped off. I thought the whole thing would pass under your radar."

"I would have let it pass, but Jean-Georges threatened to sue me," Alicia said.

Campbell sighed, slumping back down on the bed. "Believe me, Alicia, I know. And when you threatened to fight back by showing Jean-Georges your early designs, I freaked. I realized Jean-Georges would know I'd stolen them to impress him. So with my marriage on the line, I saw my opportunity during the mob scene at the store last Friday, and I sneaked in. I hid in the storage room until everyone left."

"Did you come down from Chicago for the sale, or

specifically to tamper with Alicia's laptop?" I asked.

"For the sale, of course," Campbell said. "I'm a fan of the Swoon label as much as the next person."

"So your plan was spur of the moment?" Alicia confirmed.

"Totally," Campbell replied. "As I mentioned, with that crazy crowd acting up, I saw an opportunity. I figured you kept your laptop with you, and since you were spending time at Swoon 2 these days and leaving the Chicago Swoon in the care of an assistant, your laptop was probably somewhere in the new store. I was right!"

"What about PFAF?" I asked. "Did we guess right that it was just a distraction?"

Campbell nodded. "After I deleted the files and took the back-up disks, I knew Jean-Georges would be the prime suspect. So I trashed the store to put suspicion on someone else. I'd just read a magazine interview with the woman who runs PFAF, so when I saw the coyote fur, I thought, why not blame her? After I was done, I escaped through a back window."

"Why didn't you just take the computer instead of deleting the files?" I asked.

"Maybe I should have," Campbell said, considering. "But I figured a stolen computer would be missed right away, while the files and disks might not be noticed for a long time. By then, Alicia might have thought some glitch had deleted them or that she'd just mislaid the disks. Plus, it wouldn't have made sense for PFAF to steal a computer, and I wanted the crime to point to them."

"Alicia would have noticed right away that the files were missing if Jean-Georges had pressed his case," I said.

"I was planning to do everything in my power to keep him from suing her," Campbell said. "But if he went ahead, at least he wouldn't be able to see I'd taken Alicia's work." She shot Alicia a grave look. "You've got to understand. I want to keep him from suing as much as you do, especially now that you've got your files back, because if you defend yourself by using them, I'm in big trouble."

"What about the butterfly earrings?" I asked. "PFAF stealing them wouldn't make sense either. Unless Bettina wanted to raise money for her cause. But then, why not take more jewelry?"

"Stealing them was an afterthought—a careless one," Campbell said wearily. "I was tempted by them since they matched my eyes."

A man's voice, French-accented, called out from the doorway of the bedroom. "Alicia? Nancy? This is a pleasant surprise! I hear we have intruders." I turned to see Jean-Georges's suave figure standing in the doorway, flanked by two policemen.

"Hi, Jean-Georges," I said, "Alicia and I were just leaving." We said good-bye hastily and slipped by them, leaving Campbell to explain things—or not.

Back in River Heights, Alicia treated Bess, George, and me to a late-night exclusive opportunity to browse at Swoon 2 for free dresses. Ned was dispensing free advice while we modeled. I'd just chosen a sleeveless dress the color of a lime with gold sequins scattered across it. "Awesome!" Ned pronounced.

"Great with your strawberry blond hair, Nancy," Alicia added.

"I'm not sure about this dress," George said, peering uncertainly into the mirror at her image in a midnight blue silk party dress with silver beads on the bodice. "Alicia, it's really nice of you to include me tonight, since I was AWOL at lacrosse all week."

"You helped me at Mr. Tsao's house," I reminded her. "Plus, I told Alicia you could use a new dress."

"George, it's you," Ned said firmly from his armchair.

"No, *I'm* me," George protested. Then she threw Alicia a smile. "I love it, Alicia. Thanks so much."

Meanwhile, Bess was admiring herself in another mirror wearing a strapless light yellow satin dress that matched her hair. "This dress is amazing, Alicia. You are so nice to do this. Thanks."

"Well, I'm grateful to all of you—and especially to you, Nancy—for helping me figure out who the vandal was and why," Alicia said. "Now I can move forward without being paranoid it'll happen again." She threw Ned a sly look. "I haven't forgotten about your contribution to this case."

Huh? Ned? What could she possibly give Ned from her store?

Later, as Ned dropped me off at home, I found out. As we said good night, he took a tiny velvet box from his pocket. "Here you go, Nancy. From Alicia to me to you."

I opened the box, and a pair of butterfly earrings sparkled up at me. Unlike the ones that Campbell had lifted, these were light green stones, peridots. "They'll match your new dress," Ned commented with a smile.

I grinned. "Why did I ever think guys don't notice what women wear?"

"Because these earrings were Alicia's suggestion," Ned admitted. "And I was sort of winging it, giving you, Bess, and George all that advice in the store. So, okay, maybe I don't get clothes, but I definitely notice important things, like what an awesome detective you are, Nancy. And how Alicia's mystery has been solved thanks to you."

I laughed. "And thanks to you, Bess, and George. Tomorrow, maybe I can relax."

"You? Relax?" Ned asked, smirking. "Not likely!"

I playfully punched his arm—knowing he was totally right.

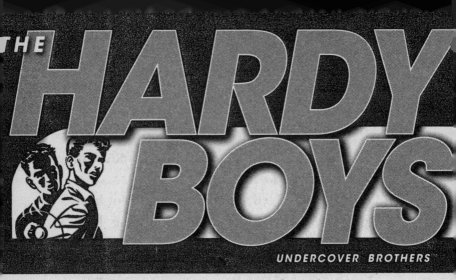

THE HARDY BOYS

UNDERCOVER BROTHERS™

They've got motorcycles,
their cases are ripped from the headlines,
and they work for ATAC:
American Teens Against Crime.

CRIMINALS, BEWARE:

THE HARDY BOYS ARE
ON YOUR TRAIL!

Frank and Joe tell all-new stories of crime,

danger, death-defying stunts, mystery, and teamwork.

Ready? Set? Fire it up!

REDISCOVER THE CLASSIC MYSTERIES OF NANCY DREW